THE WOLF OF ALLENDALE

HANNAH SPENCER

HARPER LEGEND

HarperCollins books may be purchased for educational, business, or sales promotional use. For information, please email the Special Markets Department at SPsales@harpercollins.com.

ISBN 978-0-06-267461-6

Time will be when the broadest river dries
And the great cities wane and last descend
Into the dust, for all things have an end.

GEOFFREY CHAUCER

And the end came before the beginning.

T. S. ELIOT

1

It was a portent. A terrible omen.

Bert shivered as he looked up at the strange, teardrop-shaped object in the sky. It was almost as bright as a quarter moon now. He pulled his jacket tighter around his body, although it wasn't the ever-ravaging wind that was bothering him. A strange, unsettling worry was gnawing deep inside him. His grandfather had warned him long ago about these huge fiery stars and the awful prospects they heralded.

He had a perfect view of the sky up here on the hills. He'd first noticed this thing about a week ago and had been marking its progress against the stars of Orion. It had moved since last night; that was certain.

Was this it? The sign he'd hoped he'd never see?

He stared at it, willing it to give up its meaning. Dread seized hold of him. He was too old. He couldn't do it; not now. All the long years he'd watched over these fells, waiting for it, he'd never really expected it would happen. But now, in his twilight years, the nightmare was returning. And he—an old man—was supposed to stop it.

His grandfather had told him the story, must be fifty years ago now. A story that had been handed down for countless generations. Fifty years, and he remembered it as clear as day. The day would eventually come. They'd all been certain of that.

But why now? Why him? He should be left to hand over the secret, and the onus, and live out his life in peace.

He took a deep, shuddering breath, concentrating on the frigid air burning into his throat and lungs, and looked out into the empty darkness. He knew these fells so well that even by the faint glimmer of starlight he could visualize every rock and stream. The familiar emptiness tonight seemed sinister and threatening. The cold prickled at the back of his neck. Was it out there already? Watching, waiting?

He shook his head. He couldn't be lingering on these fancies. He may yet be wrong. He offered heartfelt prayers every night that he was.

Far down the hillside he heard a whinny, probably a restless horse outside one of the town's inns. Allendale was nearly a mile away but sound always traveled well at night. He could just make out the faint glow of a lantern, maybe outside the inn itself. Nothing else betrayed the presence of the sleeping town. Most folks would be abed by now.

He heard a slight scuffle of feet and a warm furry body pressed against his shin, sitting down almost on top of his feet. Bert reached down and rubbed the top of the dog's head.

"Good boy, Shep," he murmured.

He began to walk along the stone wall running down the hillside, running his fingers along the contours of the rough-hewn blocks. Shep jumped up to follow. The sheep were all on the other side, settled for the night. He could hear the grinding of many sets of teeth on the cud and he leaned on the wall, the familiar rhythm soothing him. There were a few whispers as some of them stirred, but they all recognized him and not one stood up. There was no other sound disturbing the night; just the eternal song of silence.

Bert sighed and looked up again at the strange light in the sky. How long was it going to last?

Even if this wasn't the time, things were changing. The world was fast becoming a whole new place. He remembered when they built the railway into Catton. They were still talking about bringing it into Allendale. He could see the train from here sometimes—a hellish, ugly, belching monster. He turned his head and spat on the ground. Noise, people, machinery. A dirty, poisonous haze. Newcomers from the towns. Progress, they called it. It was awful.

Thomas had loved it. He'd looked on with shining eyes, his mouth wide when he saw the thing screech into Catton station for the first time.

"I want to drive one of those one day! Can I, Grandpa? Can I?" He tugged at his sleeve in excitement.

"You'll tend the sheep on the fells. We Allenstons have always done that, far longer than any other family." Bert smiled at the boy with quiet pride.

Thomas's face fell. "I don't want to do that. I don't like sheep; I want to drive a steam engine."

That had hurt, so much. But the boy was too young to understand.

Once, back when Bert was young, he'd traveled to Newcastle. Full of smoke, noise, dirt, and soot, it had been unbearable. Was his beloved home to go the same way?

He heard a quiet chortle behind the wall and a soft nose nudged his hand. Bert absently scratched behind Molly's ears. He'd never known a sheep so friendly. Even as a ewe lamb she'd never been at all nervous around him.

Shep sat on his haunches, his nose just an inch from his master's hand. His two companions, his friends, they had no cause for worry. They knew nothing about the coming changes. For them life would go on, as it always had and always would.

Comforted by this thought, he pushed himself away from the wall and went back up to his bothy. As he reached the door a deep, nasal honking came from far up overhead. He looked up, but of course he could see nothing. Shep was also trying to source the sound. The geese were late this year. Normally they would have arrived weeks ago.

Bert stood for a while as the sound rapidly moved south and then faded into the distance. Carried by the wind, they'd soon be miles away. Where had they come from? Where were they going? How did they always seem to know the way? He wished he knew.

Shep watched him climb into bed from the rug in the corner of the room. He never settled himself until he'd supervised his master safely into bed. It was like his two-legged ward was as much responsibility as the four-legged ones.

Bert looked over at him and noticed gray hairs around his muzzle. He must be nine years old now.

"You're getting old, boy. We're all getting old."

Shep wagged his tail. As Bert lay down and pulled the blanket over his head, his last sleepy thoughts ran through his mind.

It may not come to be.

2

They were angry. It didn't take a Druid to see that.

Bran sighed as the group struggled up the hill toward his lodge. He could see Coll was in the lead, as always. The red hair of the smith was unmistakable in the light of the blazing torches. The others he couldn't yet identify.

What was the problem now? More sheep gone? A bullock maybe—that would be a huge blow this late in the year. One napping herdsman, and the blame was brought to him.

Ever since he'd returned, after nigh on ten years away, now the fully cloaked Pennaeth of the Pridani tribe, Coll had been stirring up discord. Angry and jealous, since the troubles had started he'd been claiming Bran was inept. And some were starting to listen.

Bran planted his rowan staff in front of his feet and gripped it with both hands. The raven's feathers of his cloak flowed sinuously around his body to brush the icy ground. He would look imposing, terrifying even, especially to the younger ones. Under normal circumstances, anyone seeing him standing at his lodge entrance in his raven guise would back away, uncomfortably aware of the spirit world lingering around him.

But not so this time. He saw not a hint of hesitation in the group's approach as he looked down on them. Coll had completed some training in the Druid ways, after all. His was a very simple trick, and the smith would not be fooled. The others would take his lead.

The shadowy figures became more distinct as they struggled toward him, and as Bran studied them his earlier impatience faded. He could see that the group was huddled protectively around someone in their midst, and that those at the back were constantly glancing over their shoulders. Those who couldn't maintain the punishing pace fell back, only to push forward again almost immediately. He could now hear a desperate sob, more a high-pitched wheeze as a woman struggled for breath.

The group were snatching nervous glances at him as they neared, and Coll stared rigidly at the entrance to the stone wall. Bran fought the urge to run down to meet them.

The smith halted in front of him and the others paused a few paces behind. The crunching footsteps were replaced by the quiet fizz and spit of the torches.

Bran's eyes raked over the group, none of whom would meet his eyes, until they came to rest on Coll. The smith glared at him, betraying the merest hint of desperation and fear, and licked his lips.

"Bran, please help me."

The rasping of his voice betrayed how hard the words had been. He gestured toward the gasping woman, who was clutching something under her cloak. Her hair hung over her face and shrouded the bundle. As she regained her breath her keening became more desperate.

Bran motioned the two of them to follow, went through the outer wall, and ducked into his lodge. He mentally checked his stocks of bandages, herbs, and poultices. Yarrow for bleeding; valerian as a sedative; woundwort; self-heal. It was futile, he knew. The child clutched in his mother's arms made not a whimper.

The hides fell back against the doorway and the outside world was cut off. The pungent aroma of burning peat mingling with the rich scents of many herbs and plants made the newcomers pause, unused to the heady atmosphere. Despite the man's acute distress, Bran could see Coll's eyes flicker around the lodge.

"Place him on the bench so I can examine him."

The woman hesitated, glancing at Coll.

"He wandered from his bed!" she burst out. "I was only gone a moment! The village gate was open. When we found him—" Her words were cut short by a sob.

"It's all right, Beth," said Bran gently.

Beth began to unwrap her cloak. Coll eased the boy from her arms, looking down at the pale face that lolled backward against his massive forearm. Beth's hand pressed to her mouth. Her palm and fingers were stained red.

"Coll, put him on the bench. Quickly."

A flash of resentment crossed Coll's face before he dropped his gaze and nodded. He laid the crudely swaddled body on a fleece and stroked a finger down the ashen face.

"I tried, Bran. I tried." He choked on his words and turned aside. Bran laid a hand on his shoulder for a second before turning to the child. Healing had never come naturally to Coll. He'd be hating himself for that now.

He took a slow breath as his fears were confirmed. It was obvious the child was near the spirit world. Nearly two years old, Raith had been turning into a real handful. Beth was no match for his boundless energy now her next babe was so close. Bran studied the motionless form for a heartbeat, the chest barely flickering up and down, the already weak life force rapidly fading, and began to remove Coll's rough bandages.

Blood pulsed weakly from the gaping hole in his chest. Puncture marks showed on his arms and legs and a glimmer of white showed from his rib bones. It looked just like he'd been attacked by a wolf.

But it was no mortal wolf that had done this.

Bran noted that Raith's skin was clammy and ice-cold. In fifteen years he'd never seen a child injured so badly. There was nothing at all he could do.

"I will compress the wounds with yarrow to stop more blood leaking," he said. "And then they can be sewn closed."

But even as he spoke, the boy shuddered and the feeble breath stopped.

3

No one had yet seen it, except for a faint flickering shadow, skulking in the remotest corners of the fells. But it was out there, somewhere.

Bran looked down on the village below his lodge, where the first cold rays of sunlight were alighting on reed thatch and plumes of smoke, and then turned his gaze beyond to the interminably stretching landscape of rising and falling hills. There were three dozen settlements under the ward of the Pridani, the most distant nearly four days' journey away, and it was no surprise that the beast had so far targeted only this one. It had always been the Pennaeth's village, the symbolic heart of his tribe.

He looked along the hill line toward the northwest, to where he could just make out the gleaming walls of another settlement, four thousand paces distant. Seven were in direct sight of his lodge; any problem and the smoke of the signal beacons, or the flames at night, would immediately inform him. The beacons of the more distant places could be seen from at least one of these seven, so a message could be easily relayed. It was an intricately connected web of life, all centering on this spot, the lodge of the Pennaeth.

The air was still, the calm of dawn. The faintest touch of wind stroked his face with a chill finger. He listened to the silence, the song of the earth, and the silence began to speak. He heard a silent buzz in the air, the chatter of finches as they bathed in the shallows of the faraway river. Even more distant, the whistling cry of a buzzard. A laughing child, called home for breakfast. The swish of the quern on grain. The blarting of sheep released from their fold as they searched for the first bite of grass. The song of silence, the song of life.

He closed his eyes and felt down to the heartbeat of the land beneath his feet. Pulsating currents ran through its veins, harmonizing the villages, the hills, the stone monuments of the ancients. This was the beating heart of the Pridani, in so many ways.

The energy rose up though his feet. As he breathed in the chill air, yet to be warmed by the still-weak sun, he pulled the current higher. It flooded through his veins and his nerves, filling his entire body until it streamed out from his fingertips to continue its eternal journey.

He felt the entirety of existence coursing through him, filling him, *being* him. He became the heartbeat of the fells, the heather and gorse, the birds, deer, wolves, and hare; the constant cycling of the sun, wind, and rain; the men, women, and children who depended on them. He became the whole.

At last, he opened his eyes. The spell was broken. He returned to himself. A man, whose people depended on his skill and wisdom.

He skirted the wall surrounding his lodge until he could see toward the south. There lay another threat. One very different to the beast, but potentially much more devastating. Were the two linked? He was sure of it.

A harsh screech made him look up. A kite was soaring above his lodge, and he retraced his steps to keep it in view. The bird glided down across the valley, its wings and peculiar forked tail fanned outward for balance. It dropped out of view and Bran squinted to catch it again as it swooped up the slope opposite. It drew back its wings and dropped down to settle on the Clenched Fist.

Legend told that the Goddess had formed a human fist and turned it into stone. Stone was the symbol of death. Bran, along with every Druid, had studied the animal bones and seashells that had turned to stone after life. The Goddess placed the fist on the fell high above the village, where no one would fail to see it, an eternal reminder of the transience of life. A gentle warning that all things—man and beast, plant and rock, however permanent they may seem—would eventually reach an end.

Bran studied the distant bird that was now preening on the knuckle of the forefinger, recalling the first time he'd heard that story and, years later, the first time he'd fully understood it.

He picked up a flicker of movement on the distant hillside left of the Clenched Fist, narrowed his eyes, and concentrated. A red deer stag: he could just make out the massive antlers.

As he watched the animal pick its way through the heather, he could feel its strain and exhaustion, could imagine the tremble in its legs as it struggled onward, head hanging low. A King Stag, driven from his herd by the greater stamina and strength of a younger rival, now outcast until death.

A chill finger ran down Bran's spine. The kite, and then the stag. It was a sign, a forewarning of what was to come. The wheel of life would ever turn, and there would always be some who were crushed beneath its weight.

He looked down at the village again, watching tiny figures moving about their daily life. A scene of today, of yesterday, but of tomorrow as well?

Let it not be them, he prayed. *Let them continue as they are.*

If you let them, the wind whispered in his mind.

The stag had vanished. As hard as he looked, he could see nothing now but silent rocks among the heather.

What was he to do? He was Pennaeth of the Pridani. Their life, future, and well-being lay under his guidance. Just as the stag had to fight to keep his herd, he knew that one day he would face great challenge.

And his trial was to be like no other.

He sat down on the grass, still icy and stiff on the northern side of the wall, crossed his legs, and arranged his raven cloak around his knees. The damp chill seeped through to his skin as he leaned his head against the uneven wall. He'd thought he could do it. He'd thought with his knowledge it would be easy. Raith's torn body appeared in his mind again as he stared into the distance.

It was now over two moons since the beast had first appeared. It had been the night of Samhain: that alone had told him its true nature. Samhain was the night when the veils between this world and the otherworld thinned. On this night men could inadvertently wander into the land of the Faerie, and find themselves trapped when the portal closed.

And it also worked the other way.

At first the beast had been satisfied with livestock. Cattle and sheep were found devoured. A problem, yes, but the village had prospered the last year. The losses could be suffered.

But now it was growing more daring, or perhaps more desperate. It had started taking prey from near the village, and then ventured inside the walls. A wolf could jump clear ten feet. This beast could do twice that.

The hunters had gone out, their most experienced trackers who could locate herds of deer, the lairs of wolves and bears, who could interpret every spoor and every flattened blade of grass. They'd found nothing.

There was no hunter in the land who could track the cysgod-cerddwr.

A shout and movement below. He saw a team of six hunters appear for yet another fruitless foray, four of them each hanging onto a brace of massive hunting dogs. A group of children atop the wall watched them go. One of these dogs could bring down a three-year stag. Two, a boar. Five would harry a bear until a spear or arrow could be loosed. How many would it take to bring down the cysgod-cerddwr? More than the eight he could see; he was sure of that.

What do you hope to achieve? he wanted to cry.

But of course they had to be doing something, however futile it was. Everyone needed that illusion of control.

He could see no red hair: Coll wasn't among them. Although he'd most likely instigated the foray, he'd be occupied with the burial of his son. Although Bran normally sung the rituals to send a soul on its final journey, all those with Druid training could do it, and Coll had wanted to sing his son's passing himself.

Bran looked up at the cloudless sky for a moment. He'd applied the standard protective measures and thought it would be sufficient to guard the village. He'd made a terrible mistake.

He took a breath as he remembered every trial he'd suffered—and survived—in his life. Every trial could be overcome. He exhaled, watching the vapor swirl and fade into the air, letting his self-doubt and worry disappear with it.

Then he smiled grimly and rose fluidly to his feet. His raven's feathers flowed around him as he began to stride down the hillside.

He would not let that mistake happen again.

4

The sounds of pick and shovel rang loud in the confines of the cave. Mick Pinkerley leaned on his shovel with his hand over his mouth, trying not to breathe the bitter air. He hated this. The filth stuck to his skin and got into his eyes as the sweat ran. He couldn't help rub them with a grimy finger. Then they stung worse than ever.

It felt like a betrayal, this job. That was the worst thing. He'd seen old Mr. Allenston as he'd walked across the fell this morning, and Mick sensed his disappointment. The old man had thought he'd be a shepherd, Mick often thought.

George Templeton was working quickly—dig, thrust, dig, thrust—as he propelled the rapidly diminishing heap of rubble into the waiting wagon. Further into the depths of the chasm, other men were already laying the charges for the next round of blasting.

George glanced back, then stopped. "Pinkerley, get a move on! We need to get done here! Boss'll be hopping mad if it's not finished yesterday."

He coughed, spat, and turned back to the heap. A half minute later he threw another glare of annoyance.

"Pinkerley! It's my wages you're wasting, as well as your own. Or have you forgotten we work as a collective?"

Mick stumbled over the treacherous floor and dug his shovel in. The last intact blister on his hand burst. A sharp pain pulsed through his left shoulder with each movement. He paused again to lick his raw palm, a futile attempt to ease the stabbing pain, and glanced back into the shadows of the cave. The dust had barely settled from the last round and the incessant activity just stirred it up even more. The single lantern barely penetrated the fug.

He looked again. Did something just move? Or was it just the flickering lantern playing tricks?

"For God's sake, Pinkerley. What's the matter?"

George's expression changed to one of mocking contempt. "Oh, poor little Micky! He's scared of all the nasty monsters! Why did Boss have to put a mine in Hell's Mouth, of all places?"

Mick's temper rose. He was fifteen, not a child. He did a man's work; why didn't people treat him like one? He threw down his shovel and began to reply, but George cut him off.

"Look, Boss wants the lead out, and even Satan himself would be hard pushed to keep him from what he wants. And this new mine's the only one left that's anything like productive. Do you want to eat boiled turnips and freeze your backside to the bone looking after sheep all your life, like that old fossil up on the hill?"

"That's Mr. Allenston. He looks out for me." Mick tried to sound stern, but it came out more peevish.

The other miners clattered back, and more than one hard stare came in their direction. Mick quickly dug in with his shovel. George was right. He'd soon been replaced if he didn't pull his weight. But Hell's Mouth, he knew the stories. Everyone did. What if they were true?

The footsteps died away, leaving only a deafening silence that rose from deep under the hillside. The reverberating scrape of the shovel somehow made it even more sinister.

He glanced uneasily over his shoulder again. The Templetons had come from away; George was an outsider. His own family had lived on the fells for generations, and centuries of unease had seeped deeply into his soul.

"George? You know the stories, right?"

"Yeah, I know," he answered between thrusts of his shovel. "A demon, locked in this cave hundreds of years ago. If it's disturbed, it'll escape and wreak havoc. You really believe that?"

He didn't wait for an answer. "I know what I believe in. Money. And the boss's boot up my backside." He stopped midthrust.

"Hey, look at that, Micky!"

George dropped his shovel and crouched to inspect the partially uncovered stone.

"It's got really strange eyes; they look alive."

Mick looked at the discovery with horror. It was a wolf. Evil, pure evil. He felt sick.

"Don't touch it!" he shouted, but it was too late. For a split second he felt dizzy, as if an immense black shadow swept over him before vanishing out of the cave. The lantern guttered and almost died. There was a bitter taste in his mouth, caused by more than the ever-present lead dust. He had the strange impression he could hear a raven's warning screech.

George held the stone head out toward him. "See how its eyes are glittering? Maybe they're diamonds or something." He grinned.

"Perhaps we should put it back . . ."

"No way! I found it, I'm keeping it. The missus is having a baby soon," he added. "I need the money."

Mick forced himself to touch the head. George held on to it for a second, then relinquished it.

It was just a lump of stone, that was all. It was cold in his hands and left a residue of dust on his fingers. He felt ashamed of his panic. No wonder they all treated him like a child. There was nothing sinister about it at all.

He studied the eyes. "They just look like stone, like the rest of it. There's nothing valuable there."

George snatched it back, turned it over, then looked suspiciously at his companion. Mick held his hands out, palms upward.

"It must have been the lantern light, then," he reluctantly conceded. "Funny how they were sparkling, though. They were looking straight at me."

He looked at Mick once more, then tucked the head into his smock. "I'll take it home, anyway. A present for the missus. That's if she's got home from church yet." He raised his eyebrows. "All Souls' Day today."

"All Souls' Day? What's that, then?"

"God knows." George grinned at his own wit.

5

The sheep were restless. They could sense it too.

Bert could hear shuffling movement on the other side of the wall. There were no peaceful teeth on the cud. He leaned on the wall—the icy moisture in the crevices biting through his sleeves—hoping that his familiar presence would soothe them and that they would soothe him. Shep whined quietly by his feet, the sound almost masked by the gusting wind.

The eerie light was brighter than ever; it was getting closer. The beast was coming, he knew it. Something was to disturb it from its prison after who knew how long. It would be savage, desperate, incomparable to any earthly creature. With a surge of fear, dread, doubt, and a little pride, he resolved to prepare himself. It would be the biggest challenge of his life.

He hefted his crook in his hand. The familiar weight gave him confidence although he knew it would be of little use. His fingers traced the contours of the horn handle he'd carved. Although worn smooth over the years, the original shape was still clear. People always assumed it was a dog he'd carved, but in truth it looked more like a wolf.

There was no point trying to sleep. He was wide awake and myriad thoughts were tumbling through his mind. He settled himself on the smooth stones near the sheepfold, arranged to form a near comfortable seat out of the prevailing wind, and tucked his smock about himself. Then he began to recall everything his grandfather had taught him so many years ago.

His grandfather had learned it from his father, and he from his father before him. It had been passed down for God alone knew how long, but he knew the secret was old. Very old.

But then, the hills had long memories, as did those who lived among them.

He thought through everything that was known about the beast. Its nature, where it had come from. What would deter it, and what would be useless.

And then, finally, every detail of the ritual he would have to perform to capture and imprison it. This was the most important bit—his grandfather had stressed how imperative it was that the ritual be followed to perfection—and Bert ran through it four times before he was satisfied.

The half-moon drifted across the sky, then bid him good night as it descended behind the distant fell. The bright stars of Sirius and Orion's Belt took its place. The wind quieted. Lost in the world of the past, his hands tucked into his coat and his feet growing numb, Bert caught a whiff of what smelled like his grandfather's tobacco. The scent took him straight back to that fateful day, and the long-ago memories began to rise.

He saw himself as a young boy, even younger than Thomas, sitting at his grandfather's feet in this very same spot. It was the day he'd grown up. The day he'd learned the true meaning of responsibility.

One day, he too would have to pass on the secret. But to whom? Who would remember the old ways in years to come? Thomas wasn't interested; he was a child of the new century. For him, life was all about the future, not the past.

Maybe he was to be the last of a chain unbroken for millennia. The thought saddened him. Maybe that was why the prophecy was awakening now, in the twilight of his life.

As he gazed up at the sky he heard, far in the distance, a sound. Faint enough to pose no immediate threat, but it was a threat nonetheless. The sheep heard it too, and a ripple of frightened blarting ran through the flock.

He'd never heard it before in his life, and neither had his sheep, but the sound was buried deep in all their unconscious memories. It was the howl of a wolf.

And it was hunting.

6

Bran nodded approvingly as he approached the village. The sunlight bounced off the courses of stones that made up the wall, solid and imposing. The ditch at its foot gleamed with freshly exposed silt. Both nearly five hundred paces in length, it had taken almost two moons' work involving nearly all men, women, and older children to get this far.

Neglected for nearly two generations, storms and wind had driven soil and debris into the ditch to the point where it was possible to simply walk over it. And the wall had crumbled, its stones reused, until the gates had become an unnecessary delay.

Bran touched the raven's skull amulet hanging at his throat. The winter had been mild so far, and the snows had held off. Last year the Cailleach had risen early from the bitter north. Even before the Hunter had appeared in the eastern sky, the Goddess had changed her aspect from Mother to Crone, from summer to winter, and had buried the fells deep in snow.

But of course, every blade was sharpened on two sides. What aided them also aided their foe.

He squelched over the bank of cleared silt to look down the steep sides of the ditch. His boots sank into the sludge, and a trickle of displaced gray water ran over them, but because his boots were made of thick cowhide, coated with birch resin and beeswax and stuffed with sheep's wool, he didn't feel the dampness at all.

The water was now the depth of a man's waist and would be twice that after a couple of the Cailleach's blizzards had fallen and melted. The Goddess in her winter guise would not leave her people undefended. It was now necessary to use the single causeway leading to the oaken gate to access the village. He could see it from here, flanked by the two stone heads that he himself had carved. A red deer hind and a hare. Not only did they watch over the village but they offered a sense of pride to locals and visitors.

Bran traced the line of the wall. He struggled to see even a plume of smoke rising above it. They'd raised it higher than it had ever been. Combined with the ditch and the earthen bank, it was a greater height than two tall men.

But there was still a lot to do. Too much. He glanced toward the south and hoped they'd done enough.

He walked along the ditch bank, heading toward the rhythmic scraping of picks and shovels and the swoosh of emptying pails.

Four young lads and two girls on the verge of womanhood were hacking away at the accumulated silt and debris, shoveling it into baskets. He smiled to himself. He could tell from their studious concentration that they were all too aware of his inspection.

He waited. Not one of them glanced in his direction.

Their baskets were soon full, and after a hopeful attempt to pack them a little tighter, the group shared a quick conferring glance and one of the girls was silently elected to empty them.

She boosted the heavy load into her arms and reluctantly turned toward him, flicking a quick glance at him before concentrating on her bare feet, caked in thick mud that had splashed up to her knees.

She picked a way up the slippery slope with exaggerated attention. He could see the sheen of sweat on her face despite the chill air. She was a good worker, Gwen. He could see her on the Trydydd, the three most senior members of the Pridani after himself, someday.

"Good work, Gwen," he said as she reached the spoil heap. "Well done."

She hesitated, struggling for a response, then her hand slipped off her muddy basket. She made a futile attempt to grab it but it clipped her knee and overturned. Silt and mud splashed everywhere, coating her already filthy feet and shins, then speckling over his raven cloak. A gasp of horror came from the ditch, and Gwen's mouth froze open in dismay.

"Be thankful the ground isn't frozen," he continued. "In the past I've dug ditches where we had to have fires burning to keep the ground soft enough to dig."

Gwen nodded hesitantly, her eyes still riveted to his spoiled cloak.

"But anyway, I hear you are betrothed," he said, smiling. "I'll look forward to seeing you at the spring ceremony."

He knew she'd smile then, both shy and happy. The smile of youth and love.

"I'm really looking forward to it, too." She blushed and pushed a strand of hair back from her face, leaving a smear of mud across her cheek.

He squeezed her shoulder. "Carry on, else you'll get cold. It's still a chill wind for wearing knee breeches and short sleeves."

She picked up her empty basket and hurried back to the ditch.

"Thought he'd turn you to stone for doing that," Bran heard as he walked away, and he chuckled to himself.

A shout came from near the river, the direction the hunters had gone earlier. A dog barked. The short, excited bark that informed the hunters that a trail had been found. What had they got? Bran strode toward them.

One of the hunters noticed him, and they all turned to face him while he was still a hundred paces away. Even the dogs waited quietly. Still no Coll.

The two younger ones stepped back from the path, eyes nervously on the ground. It was the older men Bran was more concerned with. More worldly, if no wiser, he could sense a resentment in their attitude. Their eyes were dropped from sullenness. He saw one's lips move but couldn't hear what he'd said.

The only one who would meet his eyes was Fearn, who had climbed down the riverbank a short distance away. Bran smiled and nodded. As he'd intended, the friendly gesture to an equal was not lost on the other hunters.

"Prints," Fearn stated as Bran jumped down the bank. He indicated the dark mud, already softened by the sun. "I noticed two bent stems of grass farther up. Although they'd sprung back upright, the stems were slightly crushed in this direction. So I searched down here, and found the prints near the riverbank."

Bran looked down. Four toes and four claws, just like a wolf.

Except these were huge. The width of a man's hand span. They headed to the edge of the seething water and then vanished.

Either the beast could swim, or it had jumped. The river was fifteen paces across.

There was a murmur from the rest of the group as they came down the bank. Many glanced round as if expecting the beast to reappear any moment.

It won't, Bran thought. Not until it's ready, and that won't be when you are.

He crouched to study the prints closer. A wave of dizzy nausea struck him. The prints seemed to flicker, pulsate as if the perpetrator were still walking invisibly along the bank. He couldn't tear his eyes away.

A black miasma swirled out toward him. He could feel it seeping around him, creeping into his soul and his mind. He felt his soul cringe under its touch, cornered like a field mouse before a hawk. He'd never encountered a cysgod-cerddwr before, and for the first time, he realized exactly what it would mean.

The world shrank to nothing but that terrible residue of malevolence. He was aware of a tight throbbing in his temple, faster and faster. His breath was like shards of ice in his chest. Before he'd even faced the beast, it had beaten him.

Screeching ravens, far away. Dancing flames. Three forged iron birds stepped around on their posts to glare down on him. Terror surged through him. He began to fall.

The spell the cysgod-cerddwr had wrapped around him was shattered by the movement. The riverbank, the sticky mud, the worn rocks, reappeared. He could again hear the rattle of the current. He caught his balance just before he landed on his knees.

He focused on a reed swaying up and down, up and down, as the water relentlessly buffeted it. One breath. Two. The icy grip of panic faded. His heart settled. The shadow was burned out of his soul by the fire of his spirit. He swallowed hard, his throat as parched as midsummer heather.

He pushed himself to his feet, forced himself to focus as another wave of dizziness washed over him. He dug his nails into his palms. The sharp pain drove away the last remnant of shock. He composed his face, and only then turned to face the group.

All were looking at him, puzzled. A couple of them glanced at the prints. Why did they not sense what he had? He knew the answer at once.

It was a message intended for him alone. A warning, a taunt, a display of power. A statement that it was here, and there was nothing he could do about it.

It had crossed the river. Otherworldly beings did not—could not—do that. Water was an inviolable boundary. Just what was this thing?

He became aware that he was staring at nothing. Fearn stepped forward, concern etched on his face.

"Where is Coll?" Bran asked before the other man could speak. "Has he finished the burial ritual?"

There was silence. The hunters glanced at each other and Fearn looked awkward.

"Well? Speak to me, Fearn."

Fearn looked at him levelly and Bran regretted his sharp tone. The two younger boys, with barely two or three hunting forays completed, tried to discreetly slip away, no doubt imagining a shower of lightning bolts or such like. Everyone watched them go.

Fearn waited until the sound of their scrabbling had died away. "He is making talismans to try and drive the beast away. He says you have not done enough. He says iron is the only way to banish it."

Bran's hands tightened on his staff. He had the sense he was sliding, like a child down an icy hillside, helpless and out of control. Everyone looked at his white knuckles and another man retrieved his dogs and backed away.

"All possible measures are already in place," Bran informed his remaining audience, his words clipped and clear although seeming to come from outside himself.

He took a sharp breath and concentrated on the men. "Our ancestors are walking among us. I have called on them to guard us and watch over our steps."

As he'd expected, this provoked a superstitious shiver. Two men glanced behind them and made the protective gesture against the evil eye. The spirits were around them at all times, unseen and unheard, and they were at Bran's behest. What whispering, what clandestine thoughts would they be reporting back to him?

"The knot of life has been woven around the village in an unbreakable barrier that nothing can cross." He paused deliberately.

"Coll is a master ironworker, that's true. But he has no experience in controlling the spirit world."

More worried gestures. Coll's soul and personality seemed to mirror the blazing furnace with which he spent his days. Likely the reason for his incredible talent. But this was also the reason behind his much-resented failure to become cloaked, despite his years of Druid training. He'd never learned to temper his fiery nature with the other elements.

Fearn was still looking uneasy. There was obviously something else as well. Bran held his gaze, forcing him to speak.

The hunter licked his lips and took a step back. "He thinks a better Pennaeth is needed."

Bran froze. His anger rose, both at the challenge and at his own weakness. As he exhaled, it pulsed out in a swirling cloud. One of the dogs yelped.

A smith plied one of the most respected crafts, and if he were Pennaeth besides . . . It would elevate the status of the Pridani immeasurably.

Coll could not become Pennaeth, not unless he were cloaked. There were two ways to do this. The first was to be awarded a cloak by another cloaked Druid, as he himself and almost all Druids had been. The second way only happened rarely now. That was to capture the cloak of a Druid in a battle.

In old times when the Pennaeth was challenged, a battle to the death followed, and the vanquished's blood nourished the soil to bring in the new era. Just like the King Stag. Just like the perpetual death of the God of the Green every autumn. But now, the change was down to popular opinion. The supplanted Pennaeth was simply driven out.

A shout broke the tension. A girl was tearing down the track from the village.

"A messenger! A messenger is coming!"

7

"Who is coming? From which direction?"

"A rider. From the south, a thousand paces distant. I think it's the man who came before." The girl panted out her news as fast as she could, looking between Bran and Fearn.

Her eyes widened as she remembered who she was talking to, and she stepped back almost fearfully as she searched Bran's face.

"Thank you, Mintana. You've done well." Bran deliberately turned toward the village and put a hand on her shoulder. He wondered what news Don was bringing. How close the warriors were getting. "How's your archery coming along?"

The girl kept pace at his side. "Um . . . they say I'm doing well. That I've got natural talent. And I've been making my own bow as well. And when Seb cut himself on an arrow blade, I poulticed it with yarrow and bandaged it, all by myself."

The girl seemed to grow in both height and confidence as she spoke, looking up at him for approval.

Bran smiled indulgently. "Perhaps in a couple of years you could come to me as my apprentice, learn the healing craft. What would you think to that?"

Mintana's mouth fell open. "Do you really mean that?!"

"Certainly. You've obviously got a natural affinity for healing—not all people do—and as you know my last apprentice left at midsummer to start his years as a Wanderer. And perhaps afterward you could do Druid training proper."

Her face broke into a grin. Everyone aspired to the Druid craft.

"That'd be brilliant! Ma and Pa will be so pleased!"

She glanced toward the village walls, no doubt wondering who was watching.

Bran gestured forward. "Off you go, then, lass. Keep working hard, and we'll talk more about it in the spring."

Mintana nodded seriously then blushed pimpernel red. She raced on up the path with the infinite ease of youth, arms pumping wildly.

Fearn stepped up to his side. "She, at least, will be ever loyal to you now," he murmured.

Bran shook his head impatiently. "The children need encouragement. That is why I encourage them. Don't think I'm playing a petty game of strategy and ally building."

Fearn spread his hands out in apology. "Don is here already; look."

The stocky pony was trotting down the last incline toward the swelling crowd outside the gate. Bran and Fearn reached the village walls just as Don was swinging down from its back. People stepped back to let them through.

"What news, Don?" Bran clasped hands with him. A boy took hold of the sweating pony's forelock and led it toward the river to drink.

"A lot to discuss. But first I need mead. Even in winter, riding is thirsty work." He wiped his face with his cloak.

"Mintana, bring mead!" Fearn shouted to his pupil. "And bread and meat, to the Meeting Hut."

The girl raced off.

"You've finished fortifying the walls," Don observed as they passed over the causeway, observed by the hind and the hare. "You've worked hard this last moon."

"I hope it is enough."

Don shook his head and made a futile gesture. "Walls, ditches, gates, they're nothing to them. They just smash through them.

Everyone I've spoken to in the south, they say they've never come across anything like them, neither in living memory nor in the Histories. It's like the war with the Fomorii, only much worse. We've got a big problem, that's for sure."

Bran looked up at his new walls, which suddenly seemed weak and insubstantial. He'd feared as much in his darkest moments. The Pridani were strong. They would fight, and the Gods would fight beside them. He would make sure of that.

But what of their foe, and their own Gods?

He glanced up and saw a skein of pink-footed geese overhead, flying south. What did that mean? They came from the north, from the land of ice and the realm of the dead, going in the direction in which *they* were. A good omen? Or not?

The three men wove between the low-eaved buildings. A woman pushing her quern stone back and forth sat back and glanced up at them, reaching for the dish she was filling with flour. Coll and Beth caught up with them a moment later.

They reached the Meeting Hut at the far end of the settlement, a little away from the dwelling huts. Mintana was already outside, a clay jug of mead, some bread, and a chunk of cold mutton proffered on a wooden platter.

"Thank you. Off you go."

She looked disappointed as she went away, looking back hopefully as Bran ducked through the door drapes.

Don followed him inside, Coll, Beth, and Fearn behind. The three of them made up the Trydydd, the most senior leaders of the community after himself. Fearn was an adept hunter on whom the village owed many a full belly. Coll was a master smith and Druid trained besides, an automatic choice despite his fiery nature. Beth, the daughter of the previous Pennaeth, was respected for her careful wisdom.

Women often possessed greater insight than men, Bran mused as he dropped dry branches onto the peat embers in the hearth.

How often had a problem he'd wrestled with for an age been solved by a woman? It came from their intimacy with the threads of life, with the Goddess. There were some things no man could know. His eyes lingered on Beth's swollen stomach as she dropped to a stool. Fearn began to untie the door drapes.

Beth was looking pale and seemed to be losing weight, something which exaggerated the size of her belly. That was the hard part of a pregnancy at this time of year, when supplies of nourishing food were running short. Was there something else besides? She was grieving for Raith, obviously, but in any circumstances this would be a particularly hard babe to carry.

Fearn dropped the hide drapes over the entrance. The air grew thick and close from the smoldering peat. Shadows danced from the tallow lamps.

The gathered faces waited expectantly as Bran lifted a cup and slowly poured the mead, watching the amber liquid dance in the firelight. It seemed to split and branch like the tines of an antler, and he thought again of the King Stag struggling through the heather.

Like the battle with the Fomorii, Don had said. The Fomorii had been the original inhabitants of the land, the ones who had laid out the stone circles and monoliths that were still revered by the Pridani. It was the Pridani's own forebears who had come to this land, generations before, and claimed it for themselves, but not before a long, devastating war had been fought.

Was it now their own time to fall beneath the wheel of time and change? Were they now to succumb to the next wave of invaders as a new cycle began? Bran handed Don the filled cup with a sense of foreboding. The messenger drained it in a gulp and held it out for more.

Coll unsheathed his knife and severed a large piece of the mutton with one deft slice. He speared it with the blunted end and began to chew, the firelight pulsing over his stubbled chin. It was a knife of his own design. Very cleverly made, Bran had to admit; ideal for both carving and eating.

He noticed Don take a step closer to the smith, discreetly observing the unusual tool. No doubt he'd be memorizing the design for the smith in his own village.

"I see you've finished the sentinels for the gate," he said to Bran. "You've captured a remarkable likeness to life. I've not seen comparable work anywhere else at all. May their souls guard you well."

A subtle gesture of diplomacy; Bran expected nothing less. He smiled an acknowledgment, both of the compliment and the reason behind it. Don bowed his head.

"Three moons' work. Five blades, three chisels, endless blistered fingers." Bran chuckled. Everyone smiled except Coll, who was deliberately concentrating on his meat.

"Tell me. With the deer, why did you choose the hind and not the stag?"

Don was looking at him with genuine interest. It was a good question. It was the stag who battled throughout the autumn, after all. His life was defined by defense of his right. But until now, nobody had asked him why he'd chosen the gentle hind.

"The stag fights," he said quietly. "He fights for his pride. For his bloodline. He fights for the defeat of his rival."

Bran studied the faces of his audience. Outside, a child shouted. Coll went to the table, cutting himself a new chunk of meat. His careful concentration showed he was also listening.

"But the hind; she will also fight. She fights for her children and will defend them to the death. The hind fights for love, for life, for the future. It is the female who is the vessel of life. The male is only the vessel of death."

His eyes lingered on Beth and her swollen stomach a moment longer.

Don stretched his arms back, cracking his shoulder joints. "A most interesting choice. It speaks the full wisdom of the Druids." He smiled his respect.

A piece of wood collapsed in the hearth, sending up a fizz of sparks. The atmosphere changed, grew expectant. It was time to begin the real purpose of the meeting.

8

Shep was staring at the door, his ears pricked and alert. Then his tail began to wag. Bert took a sip of his tea. So far he hadn't heard anything, but he had a good idea who was coming.

A couple of minutes later, just as he put his mug down and bent to pull on his boots, the door flew open, admitting an icy blast of wind. The smoke swirled from the hearth and a puff of ashes eddied into the room.

"Howay, lad, shut the door!" He grinned conspiratorially at his grandson. "Shouldn't you be in school?"

Thomas grinned back as he dropped onto the stool near the door. "I won't tell if you don't."

"I'm getting the other ewes in-by this morning, back from Gaterley Hill, and sorting out the ones for market. Then the rams can go in with the rest, ready to lamb next spring."

He knelt awkwardly to lace his boots. The split in the left one was getting worse, he noted. Unmendable. He'd have to see about getting a new pair. He wondered if he could afford it, but wet feet was a sure recipe for pneumonia.

"They should have been sorted out two weeks ago," he contin-ued. "But it doesn't matter. I've a feeling it'll be a cold spring." He glanced sideways at the boy. "Lucky you happened to call in today."

Thomas shuffled on his stool. "Well, you said you were going to do it this week, and what with there being no fog this morning . . . I thought you'd like the help."

Bert chuckled and clapped him on the shoulder. What use was school, anyway? He'd never been himself, and he could teach the boy far more than he'd learn in there.

He looked critically at him while he was tickling Shep. He was filling out across his shoulders; he'd be a man soon. Tough and strong, but wiry with it. Perfect for this job.

Thomas suddenly looked up, then grinned as he met Bert's indulgent expression.

"Shall we head off, then, lad?"

Thomas jumped to his feet and they headed out the door. They went up the slope, past the outcrop shaped like a hand with the fingers folded in—the Fist, it was called—and onto the steep drove lane to the open fells.

Thomas leaped up atop the wall. He shaded his eyes and pointed. "I can see them, Grandpa! Over on yonder fell! Shall I take Shep and fetch them?"

Bert leaned on his crook as he looked. "Go on then, lad." He coughed as he caught his breath. How nice it was to have some young legs to help.

"Come on Shep!" Thomas whistled.

The dog looked up at Bert, his ears pricked in a question.

"Go on, boy." He gestured toward the white dots grazing on the far hillside, and the dog turned and headed along the track twisting through the heather.

Thomas set off at a run and Shep kept pace at his side. Within a few minutes they'd covered the half mile, and the sheep were already bunching together. Bert watched wistfully as he flexed his right knee a few times. It stiffened so easily these days. He used to be able to run like that.

The sheep were racing back toward him, boy and dog behind. Thomas was sure-footed and quick. Bert could see him leaping between the tussocks with ease, arms out for balance. He nodded, pleased with the boy's fearless attitude. If you hesitated, that's when you turned or even broke an ankle.

He'd been a champion runner himself, back in his day. The annual race for all the Dales shepherds—over twenty miles across fell and dale—he'd won six years running. Thomas should enter next year. He could probably win it.

He could hear the rumble of several hundred hooves echoing through the ground. A skylark flew up, disturbed by the commotion, and hovered over his head singing wildly. His grandfather had told him the bird always sang in the face of danger. It showed how strong and confident it was; it didn't even need to stop singing to guarantee its escape.

A second later the melody was lost as the first sheep passed. They thundered down the well-trodden track and past the Fist. They knew exactly where they were going.

They seemed keener than ever today, Bert thought uneasily. Were they also aware of the danger lurking in the hills? He would graze them closer to home, he decided. The weather would turn soon, anyway.

He walked alongside the stragglers and scanned over them for any signs of injury or ill health. He could see nothing amiss. The very last, with Thomas and Shep close at her heels, was slightly lame, but that was no reason for concern.

Thomas hopped from side to side as they walked back together. His eyes were shining and he wiped a trickle of sweat from his forehead. Bert remembered the feeling of exhilaration after racing through the fells.

Within ten minutes they had the sheep penned up in the fold. The sheep grazing on the other side were alert to the newcomers' arrival, ears pricked and noses raised to scent the air. Both shepherds laughed when a ewe's head and shoulders appeared above the wall, as she jumped up to inspect the new arrivals.

"Is that Molly?"

"Aye, it is!"

Bert was proud Thomas had managed to recognize her. His bellwether's left ear was crooked, and there was a patch of white on the side of her face, which made her easily recognizable.

She chortled and he scratched behind her ears. Thomas went to do the same but she jumped down.

"She doesn't like me!"

"She's just not used to you. She'll soon get to know you."

Bert climbed over the gate into the fold and Thomas hopped over after him, looking around with the practiced air of a seasoned shepherd. That was the only thing he'd managed to perfect so far.

"We'll sort out those that are good to breed next year. The last of this year's lambs will go to Hexham. Their pastures by the river are ideal for fattening them, far better than up here. And the old ewes that can't breed again, the butcher in town will buy."

Thomas hung on every word. "How do you get them to Hexham?"

"We walk."

Ten miles each way, it was an easy day's work.

"Maybe they could go on the train? That would be much easier." Thomas pursed his lips. "How fast does a train go? We could be there in about half an hour!" He broke into a smile. "Maybe when I learn to drive one, I'll take them up for you."

"Look, lad, we walk them. We've always done that." Hadn't the boy forgotten these ridiculous fancies by now?

"But the train would be much quicker, much easier, what's wrong with it?"

To his dismay, Bert could think of no answer.

9

"Why not this ewe?"

"She's getting old. You can feel her backbone, see?"

Thomas obliged and nodded as he felt the sharp knobs of the spine.

"She's not done well this summer, and won't manage to rear lambs again. And I bet I know why." Bert caught hold of the ewe's head and pulled her lips back. "See, she's lost her teeth."

Thomas bent down to inspect the bare gums.

"She'll find it almost impossible to graze now, that's why she's thin. She'll most likely not survive when the snows come down. It's no life for them up here when they're old and weak, she needs to go to the butcher now."

He scratched the ewe's head, who was looking up at him trustingly. He could see from Thomas's face what he was thinking.

"But . . ."

"The most important thing, lad, is to keep your sheep well and happy. It's easy to want to keep them on, especially when they're your friends, but then they just suffer a lingering, unhappy death. You've failed in your responsibility then. She's done well, but her time has come."

Thomas's eyes raked over the old and thin ewe. He nodded and rubbed behind her ears. "I understand."

"Her grandam won me the champion prize at Allendale Show one year. And that little ewe with the broken horn's her daughter. There's three more of hers somewhere."

"That's nice. It means there's still something left of them when they go, doesn't it?"

Bert looked at the boy with pride as he leaned on his crook, easing the weight off his stiff leg. He'd hoped he'd understand that. He'd placed a lot of hopes on his only grandson's shoulders. He was a sharp boy, intelligent, despite all the nonsense about train driving. He was going to do well on the fells, and so he should. The shepherd's instinct was generations bred into him. Once he settled into his life, he wouldn't look back. Bert was confident of that.

"Why are you looking at me like that?" Thomas paused as he dragged the hurdles around.

"Just thinking how nice it is that you're here. Forgive an old man his rest." He winked and Thomas grinned back as he tied the gate.

The rest were ready to turn out, and Bert ran an approving eye over them. They'd done well over the summer and would produce a good crop of lambs next year.

"The rams are in the lower paddock. We'll drive them up now and they can all go together. We'll have the ewes lambing in five months' time, in midspring. Hopefully after the snows have melted."

Thomas gave a halfhearted laugh and kicked at a stone. His earlier cheerfulness had evaporated.

Bert knew why. The boy was frightened of the rams. A ram had been responsible for his father's accident.

As he walked down the hill he thought back to that day, the day when the centuries-long chain of Allenston shepherds had nearly been broken. He'd been moving the rams up that day too. Guy, not much younger than Thomas is now, had been waiting in the fold when one charged him, crushing him into the wall. His leg was badly broken and had never mended properly. A battering ram hadn't been named as such for nothing. Guy had been forced to forgo the shepherd's life to drive a carrier's cart to and from Hexham.

Bert looked over his shoulder. Thomas was still by the fold, pretending he hadn't noticed him leave. It was only natural that he was frightened, but he was nearly a man now. Accidents happened; that was the way of life.

"Look sharp, lad," he shouted. "I want them in today!"

Thomas shuffled down toward him, studiously studying a flurry of pipits as they tumbled through the air. The rams were already waiting at the paddock gate. There came a deep, throaty chortle and then a harsh *thwack* as one gave the gate an experimental push. Thomas knelt and untied then carefully retied one boot, then the other one.

"Fetch them out, lad."

Bert leaned on his crook. Thomas looked up pleadingly, and he met his gaze impassively.

"Can I take Shep?'"

Bert hesitated, then nodded.

Thomas carefully and slowly unfastened the gate. The four rams headed to the other side of the paddock where they watched boy and dog warily.

Thomas walked toward them, taking care to keep Shep between himself and the rams. The dog seemed to sense his fear and kept close by him.

A second later the rams ran through the gate and up the track. They knew exactly where they were going. Thomas looked utterly relieved. Bert nodded and they followed the rams up.

There was a few seconds' standoff before Molly pushed through the throng to rub noses with one of the newcomers. Then they all spread out toward the hillside, eagerly cropping the coarse grass as they headed toward the drove lane. It was always like they hadn't grazed all day.

"Look! Molly's through the gate first! Shouldn't the rams be leading the way?"

They watched as she trotted through the gate, heading toward the open fell. The rest of the flock bunched to follow.

"That's the inviolable rule of pecking order, lad. As you'll come to learn, women will always fuss over trivial things like that. Old Billy doesn't care if he's first or last through the gate, but with the ewes there's hell to pay for jumping the line. We men, you see, have more important matters to think about." They shared a superior grin.

One sheep, an old and wily ewe that Bert had debated over whether to keep, paused under an ash sapling with a few leaves still hanging onto the lower branches.

Thomas saw her eyeing up the leaves, which were just out of reach. "Stand on your hind legs, then you'll reach them!"

His amusement turned to amazement as the ewe proceeded to do exactly that. She hooked a front leg over a thin branch and her bodyweight pulled it down, pinning it to the ground as she stripped off the leaves.

She was a resourceful old girl, Bert knew. That was why he'd kept her on. He guffawed at the look on Thomas's face.

"You can call her Jack-in-the-Box. You've still a lot to learn about sheep, lad."

10

"The invaders," Bran stated. "We'd thought they'd be content with the lush fat lands of the south?"

"It seems not." Don smiled shortly. "Their masculine pride in the fight. It now appears they want everything. They're pushing farther and farther this way. Every hill and dale in the land will be under their thrall before they're finished."

The news confirmed Bran's fears. Both his meditations and his reasoning had told him the Pridani would not escape their attentions. Coll's face twisted in anger and he bunched his fists.

"Let's face it, we've had several moons' warning, which was more than the Iceni had. And we are prepared, however we decide to proceed." Bran directed these last words at Coll.

"They're making those new outposts to the north into permanent camps, although with only a few warriors. Is that right?" he asked Don.

The messenger nodded. "Just enough to make sure we remember they're there. The one at Coria especially—they can control the ford over the Tyne that way."

"And that infernal road as well!" Bran couldn't help but grimace. He and some other Druids had journeyed eastward to inspect the invaders' new construction, and he'd understood the horrific principle at once. Just as the arteries of a man carry both blood and poison deep into the body, so this *thing*, gleaming like a venomous snake in the distance, was intended to do the same.

They'd watched a small party of metal-clad warriors hastening north, the unnatural, synchronized movement of the group obvious even over the distance. None of them had believed there could be anything like these people. Not on Earth, nor in Annwfn.

What had the Fomorii's first impression of the Pridani been?

The fire began to hiss, resonating like the approach of a thousand beating wings. His raven's feathers seemed to flicker like they were coming alive. For a second he thought he could see glowing black eyes in the shadows.

"The invaders are stretched very thin." Don broke in on his thoughts. "They have taken possession of Catraeth, but as you know, the Brigantes don't take kindly to being told what to do."

He laughed humorlessly and Fearn and Beth nodded seriously. Coll wiped a smear of grease from his chin. He seemed intent on devouring the entire joint of meat.

"They must watch their backs at every step. Their water is poisoned, their huts burned, wagons stolen, horses loosed. They will soon wish they'd stayed in the south."

"Would that they had, too," Beth murmured, cradling her belly with a faraway look in her eyes. Coll moved behind her to rub her shoulders and she leaned back against his solid thighs.

"So we have our plan," Coll stated. "We must attack their new outposts. Now. While they're still weak. Raze them to the ground. If they think the Brigantes are bad . . ." He squeezed Beth's shoulder and she flinched.

Bran shook his head. "They will simply retaliate. We need to find a better way."

"You mean hide behind our new walls and ditches, cowering like beaten dogs, waiting for the nasty people to go away?"

"I didn't say that."

"You're a coward, Bran. You always were. We need a Pennaeth with strength, who can drive the enemy from our land. We'll all be dead before you do anything." Coll stepped forward, his hands on his hips emphasizing his iron-hard bulk.

The fire crackled and spat in the pronounced silence. Bran looked coolly at the man's face.

Fearn spoke first. "Bran's right. We all know what's said about these invaders. We need a clear strategy, else we'll be picked off and crushed like fleas in a fur."

Don nodded. "The more desperate they get, the more brutal. We've heard they took a dozen people from Catraeth in revenge for an attack. They were nailed to trees and left to die."

An audible gasp. Beth reached up and grasped Coll's hand. Bran went cold. Somewhere in the recesses of his mind he heard the crows flapping. The room grew darker.

Don dropped his empty cup onto the table and the spell was broken.

"But if we can't attack them, what can we do?"

"The snows are late this year. That's been to their advantage, as well as ours." Don refilled his cup and turned to face them. "But within the next few days, the weather will turn."

Bran nodded. He'd thought as much himself. "What will happen then?"

"They will remain within their forts and their huts. They will concentrate on staying warm and well fed until the spring comes and they can renew their war."

"Then we must attack at once. Drive them out. We can't have them remaining among us like a nest of lice! We are just sitting around doing nothing. Nothing!"

Coll's fist punctuated every word. And people wondered why he'd not been cloaked.

Beth levered herself up and laid a soothing hand on Coll's arm. "I don't want any more death. I'm sick of death."

Coll looked ashamed. He placed a sinewy, scarred arm around her thin shoulders.

Don smiled, his eyes hard. "Death breeds life. Life for us, and for our children. What happens when dogs are kept chained inside? They grow fat and lazy. Their teeth go blunt."

He took a hunk of bread and ripped a mouthful away. "They have never known winters like we have," he continued, his words muffled. "They have no idea of the might of the Cailleach. With her winds and snows and ice, she will drive them back. Drive them longingly to the warmth of their hearths." He swallowed and his voice rang clear as ice. "And when they at last emerge . . ." He squeezed the bread in his fist. Crumbs fell to the floor.

A log collapsed in the hearth, sending out sparks that rained down like drops of blood. Bran shuddered. None of the Pridani would pay heed to the idea that they may not defeat the invaders. There would be a few moons to reach a consensus, peaceable or otherwise, but—the King Stag came into his mind again—could it be their time which was at an end?

"We will need a stock of good weapons, then." Coll was looking thoughtful. "What weapons do they have?"

"Swords. Like ours, but smaller. They won't face a warrior in fair combat; they form ranks and lines that are unbreakable. It seems they have no champions or honor system at all. I've never had the fortune of observing them in battle, but from what I've heard, they are unnatural. Like they're not even human. Their priests, their battle magic, must be vastly superior to ours." Don glanced at Bran apologetically. "They show no fear of the war harps or the spells of the Druids. We can attack their camps with enough success, but in open battle we always lose."

Bran felt a throbbing pulse in his neck. "We must avoid battle, then. We must find a way to accept them and live together peacefully."

Beth looked at him with sudden hope. Fearn was thoughtful. But the expressions on the other men's faces told him what a difficult task that would be.

11

Bert narrowed his eyes and studied as much of the coarse, short-cropped grass as he could make out. Then he looked farther across to the higher ground. The Fist was still indistinct in the deep blue predawn light. The clouds were just beginning to emerge into visibility, sailing across the distant sky. He could see nothing amiss.

But they could.

He was so familiar with his sheep's routine that any slight change was like the alarm call of a blackbird. They should be stretching at the first hint of morning, bracing themselves to shake the night's frost from their fleeces, blarting to each other as they fanned out to seek the first bite of grass. Just as sheep had done since the dawn of time. Molly would then lead them across the burn and past the Fist, to the south-facing slope where the grass was best this time of year.

But today they were just standing in a silent huddle. Something had frightened them.

He walked to the edge of the group, his boots crunching on the frosty grass. Shep prowled along at his side, his ears pricked. He could sense it, too. Whatever it was.

"What's the matter, girls?" His voice rang loud in the silence.

A few looked back at him and stamped their feet. He walked farther. The world was now rapidly emerging from its nighttime shroud, but still he couldn't see any sign of a problem.

Shep was staring at the clump of rowans down in the valley. Bert followed his gaze and shivered.

Was it in there? Watching him?

He imagined he saw a flicker of movement in the undergrowth, but the light was still too indistinct to know for sure.

He gripped his crook harder and glanced back toward his bothy, estimating the distance and the number of seconds it would take.

But he couldn't do that. He couldn't leave his sheep.

He looked again at the rowans, searching for any more movement. Shep still hadn't moved. A single quiet blart came from somewhere behind him.

A blackbird began to sing somewhere among the trees. It was a familiar and intensely welcome sound, which at once dispelled the nightmare. The fells returned to how they should be. Familiar, safe, unthreatening. Home.

The sky was now the color of summer scabious, then an orange sheen overlaid the blue. As the cold yellow orb rose above the horizon, the spell was broken.

Molly was the first to walk slightly apart from the huddle, drop her head, and snatch a mouthful of grass. She checked to both sides as she began to chew. Gradually the others began to do the same.

A few minutes later Bert headed back inside. They'd be all right now.

A sickly, scorched smell greeted him as he opened the door. The pan of porridge he'd left on the stove had boiled dry. He ran and snatched it up, cursing as the handle burnt his fingers.

He stirred it experimentally. Most of it was almost edible. He stood at the door to eat it, his hands warm and cold from the pan and the morning air. He watched the sheep drifting down toward the burn.

He scraped the last caramelized paste from the bottom of the pan as best he could, wincing at the charred taste, then cracked the ice on his water bucket to soak it. He made a mug of tea, clutching it in both hands to warm his fingers. The rising steam mingled with his breath to form strange, twisting shapes in the air.

He looked down toward Allendale, roofs and walls glistening in the low sunshine. There was a dance on tonight, he remembered. He always enjoyed them, although of course he never danced now. Hadn't done since he'd lost his Janet. It was a chance to catch up with family and friends. Although the town was barely a mile away, he rarely made the journey, and that was mainly to see young Ellen. She was his cousin Edward's daughter, but he'd always thought of her as his niece. Especially since Eddie—known as Red Eddie on account of his hair—had died, leaving her with just her stepmother for family.

They'd always said you knew the Allenstons by their hair, and Ellen's was especially vivid. Bert's had earned him a few comments when he was younger, but it had dulled with age, and none of his grandchildren had got it. It was quite disappointing.

The sheep had long disappeared below the rise, but there were no white dots approaching the Fist. They hadn't yet crossed the burn. He drained the last of his mug and crunched across the grass. Their hooves had knocked the frost from the grass, leaving a multitude of green trails through the white. If he didn't know exactly where they were, he'd have no trouble finding them.

The sun was well-risen and he could feel the cold heat prickling on his skin, challenging the frigid air. The frost was already melting in places, but he wasn't fooled. He could hear a great tit singing, *pee-a-too-wit, pee-a-too-wit*, the peculiar tune it made only when snow was coming. He remembered his grandfather teaching him that. Come morning, winter would be properly here.

As he rounded the rise he could see them, silent and still. A few noses raised, scenting the air. The group bunched tighter.

He scanned the banks and the clumps of sedge. Nothing. A hundred pairs of eyes silently watched him. He looked closer, squatting to examine the churned mud. A multitude of hoofprints

—the shallow area was ideal for both drinking and crossing—but he could see nothing untoward. The tracks were dried and hard, segments of blue ice filling many. None were disturbed.

But they weren't happy at all.

He crossed the stream himself, hopping over the flat stones he'd laid. Decades of practice lent him balance on the icy rock. Shep hung back, watching him beseechingly.

"Come on, girls! It's all right."

Molly's nose raised slightly, scenting the air, then her ears twitched back. *No, it's not all right.*

How he wished he had their senses.

He crossed back again. His foot slipped and cracked through a layer of ice. Cold water rushed into his split boot. He shook it ineffectually. He'd have to get back and dry it out, but he couldn't leave until he knew they were happy. And there was no way he could hurry that.

As he waited, hopping on the balls of his feet as his wet toes grew numb, they gradually inched closer to the bank. They looked down at the water, and then across toward the Fist.

Molly reached the water's edge, paused, then the whole flock charged through. Ice and spray flew up to descend in rainbow droplets.

A safe distance from the burn they halted, looked back, then began to drift toward the Fist.

Suddenly, Bert was not looking forward to leaving them alone that night.

12

The Fiery Star appeared that night.

As the clouds cleared on the eastern horizon, its light shone through, surpassing even the half moon. Bran stared at it and shivered, the night air like needles on his skin. He'd seen one a few times before, but never as bright as this. It was a terrible warning. Fiery Stars always heralded devastating upheaval.

He saw from the scant few stars visible that it was slightly left of the Hunter's right foot. Did that mean anything?

The legend told that, with the reckless confidence of youth, the Hunter had tried to kill one of the Goddess's own hares, thinking what prestige the beautiful white animal would bring him when he got home.

When he pulled his arrow from the limp body, the point nicked his finger. Within seven days his arm was blackened and swollen. He was raging with fever, and on the ninth day he died.

The Goddess then raised the stars, visible from Samhain, the start of the hunting season, as an ever-present warning.

Bran was about to take on the role of hunter himself. He knelt and placed his hands on the stiff, icy stems of grass, then dug his fingers absently into the soil. The rough chill numbed his fingertips.

He had to destroy the cysgod-cerddwr, there was no other way. So why did it seem to herald such dire consequences? Had he missed something important?

Or did the warning refer to the invaders? Was it confirming his fear that a war would destroy the Pridani?

He swung back onto his heels and rose to his feet in a fluid movement, then looked south into the empty night. They were out there, shivering in their thin blankets, planning their next conquest and wishing they were back at home.

The snows were on their way. The Cailleach was waking. The Cailleach was the fourth face of the Goddess. The face of winter, the face of death.

Death for whom? The quiet thought spoke in his mind.

He recalled a legend, an ancient story about the Fomoriian war he'd heard years ago.

When the Fomorii were defeated and finally fled, they'd left something behind. A demon, their revenge on their conquerors. Its true nature was long forgotten, but he began to wonder.

Was it a coincidence that the cysgod-cerddwr had appeared just as the invaders began their relentless march north? Had it returned to see the final demise of his people, as it had once watched their arrival?

He paced the hillside, deep in thought.

All things had an end, that was true. But that didn't mean it had to be now. Events may be ordained, but the time of their passing could always be changed. The demise of the Pridani did not have to happen now. The problems of the invaders and the cysgod-cerddwr could both be resolved. He would find the way. He had been chosen for this task, and he would live up to his calling.

The breeze rippled and sang through his feathers as he moved, the rhythmic crunch of frosty grass as he circled the hilltop giving purpose to his thoughts.

Had the invaders' priests noticed the sign, too? Those purported, as Don had said, to be so much more skilled than the Druids? How would they interpret it?

Perhaps they would see it as a warning, a sign to retreat. He nursed a faint flicker of hope, but he knew it was unlikely.

The Clenched Fist, the eternal symbol of impermanence, came into view, its fingers pale and indistinct under the starlight. Its message was about to be driven home, for someone.

The wind rose and a ray of cold light, channeled by the clouds, fell on two of the boundary stones that defined the edge of the village territory, high on the fell. Placed there by the Fomorii, the same people who'd raised the monoliths and circles, they marked a boundary as old as the land. Bran traced its indistinct line, dipping in and out of sight across hummock and vale. Would it survive his lifetime? The lifetimes of young Mintana and Gwen? Their children?

The clouds drifted and the beam of light was extinguished as if his question had been answered. The breeze whipped over him, now coming from the north. The Fiery Star was obscured and the first tentative flakes of snow began to fall. Icy moisture speckled his face as he stood, motionless as the earth.

It will all work out well, he said to the night. The land and its people will know peace.

He listened, and the song of silence hummed in his ears and his mind. The only sound was the delicate fizz of snow speckling against his upturned face.

Then in the distance, carried on the breeze, he heard a howl of a wolf. Then another, and another. Mournful, hauntingly sad. They too could sense what was coming.

He pictured them far out across the moors, prowling through the heather. They weren't a problem; not unless the winter was particularly harsh.

Somewhere in the valley a sheep blarted, then fell silent. All livestock were now herded into folds or within the village walls at night, a safeguard against the fickle moorland weather and roving bands of raiders as well as the cysgod-cerddwr.

He focused his thoughts onto the immediate future and felt the heartbeat of the earth surging through his body. He felt the threads of life, of the past and future, converging on one point. A point that was soon to be.

Then a ripple of disquiet struck against him, followed by another. Harmonized as he was with the song of the earth, he could sense something approaching. Something bad.

Then the frantic barking of the hounds tore into his thoughts like an explosion of icy water.

13

Bert wanted to go home. The constant rattle from the fiddles and the drum pulsed through his skull like a blunt knife, the machinations of his distant cousin Samuel Gatesby from Catton way driving the tempo painfully higher. Bert could see the sweat running down his face as his hands bowed and danced impossibly fast, his eyes shut in concentration. He wished he could stop for just a minute.

Dancers nodded and waved as they passed, merging again into the throng before they could see his automatic acknowledgment.

The feeling of foreboding had been eating away at him all day, and more than once on the walk to the town he'd almost turned back. It was out there, and soon, soon . . .

What?

What was really going to happen? He didn't know, but what he did know was that he was far away from where he ought to be— out on the fells with his flock.

It wasn't just the beast that was worrying him. There would be heavy snow tomorrow. He'd penned the sheep into the fold before he'd left, so they should be safe, but still . . .

Shep was lying next to his feet, his head on his paws. He wasn't enjoying the evening either. He didn't much like noise, but of course Bert would never leave him at home.

He looked around and realized no one else had brought their dogs tonight. At one time there would have been a dog at every shepherd's feet, and shepherds old and young would have made up a good part of the gathering.

Shep whined softly and Bert stretched his hand down. A damp nose touched his fingers.

"You feel it, too, boy?"

Shep turned his limpid brown eyes up toward his master and they shared a long, silent look.

"Hey, a dog! Does it dance, mister?"

Bert jerked his head up. The youth was grinning down at him, his friends snickering behind. He had no idea who they were—probably come from away for work—although the young lass draped quite wantonly around the boy was Winnie Jones, the postmaster's daughter.

"You keep a civil tongue in your head, boy, when you speak to your elders and betters." Bert spat the last word.

Shep just lay still, as if the battle were already lost.

As he'd half expected, the youths weren't at all abashed. "Shouldn't it be outside, chasing sheep or something? Like you?"

Laughing, the group swaggered off into the crowd. He stared after them. Winnie turned back and he met her eyes for a second as the group merged into the throng.

He stretched his hand down again, searching for his companion's acknowledgment, and leaned his head against the wall. Why had he come tonight? He realized with a shock how many faces he didn't know, and he suddenly felt like a stranger.

The world he knew was dying. He longed to return to the fells, to Molly and his other girls. His friends. He rubbed the fur around Shep's neck and felt rather than heard the dog's deep sigh.

He caught a flash of deep orange over to the left and looked over. It was the first time he'd seen Ellen all night. It would be impossible to miss that red hair. Who was she talking to? It looked like the butcher Fred Pinkerley's son, Mick.

A half smile flickered onto Bert's face. It was obvious from the goofy look on his face that the boy was love-struck.

His smile faded. Ellen was, for who knew what reason, walking out with that wastrel Jack Felton. A looker, yes, but it was taking her far too long to see sense. And where was he tonight? He hoped, for Mick's sake, that he wasn't around. Everyone knew what Felton was like. And Mick was only—what? Fourteen? Fifteen?

A flurry of movement and like a bad penny, there was Felton. He barely needed to grip Mick by his skinny shoulder before the boy was making his escape.

Bert couldn't hear what passed between Felton and Ellen, but the girl looked on the verge of tears. Several people were watching, many more pretending not to.

Bert shook his head. The Allenstons were an old, respectable family, and Ellen was hardworking and pleasant, as well as strikingly beautiful. There was no reason why she shouldn't marry well. What on earth did she see in that worthless cad? The answer, as always, eluded him.

Felton pushed his way towards the door, leaving Ellen staring after him. As she smoothed her dress Bert's eyes were drawn to her waistline.

Wasn't that a slight thickening there?

He looked closer as her hand went to her now trembling lips. Yes, there was the start of a protruding belly, a swelling around her bosom. Damn that Felton!

He gripped the edge of the bench, wishing it was the boy's neck he was squeezing.

How long? Not long enough for it to be common gossip, thank the Lord. And obviously Felton wasn't about to do the honorable thing. Poor lass. She could have done so much better for herself.

He began to lever himself to his feet. He'd find the boy and have words with him. She had no father or brothers to stand up for her, and he was her closest relative. Cad as he was, a life in the workhouse with the other unmarried mothers would be a far worse prospect.

"Now then, Bert. How's things? Not leaving already, are you?"

Joseph Allenston, or Scruffy Joe on account of his amazingly wild hair, was the son of his father's younger brother from Wooley. Shep sniffed at his ankles.

Bert sighed and slumped back down. The prospect of a familiar and friendly face was suddenly very welcome.

"Poor turnout from the Allenstons tonight, eh? Thought your granddaughters would be here, but I saw them getting a train to Hexham, all dressed up and whatnot. Another dance there, bigger and better, they said. They don't want to stay in boring old Allendale with us!"

Bert couldn't return the lighthearted smile. Thomas's twin sisters, Claire and Rebecca, seemed to gad about all over the place. Would none of them be happy where they were?

He stared forward, his eyes struggling to take in the rapid blur of movement hurtling in front of him. He was aware of Joe studying him.

"How's the new apprentice getting on? I hear young Tom's been helping you out instead of going to school."

Bert turned to face the sly, grinning face next to him. "How do you—"

But of course everyone would know. The only difference between a secret and general knowledge was that the first would get around that much faster.

Pride made him smile. "He's doing well. Sharp, quick to learn. He's a real Allenston." He decided not to mention the steam engines.

"You'll be looking for a dog for him. My best bitch, she's just had pups. You want me to put his name on one? And how about one for yourself—this old boy's getting on now, isn't he?" Joe bent and scratched Shep's head.

The thought hurt. Bert had had many dogs over his life, but the idea of a replacement for poor old Shep, it felt like the utmost betrayal. Shep was to be his last. He'd felt that for a long time.

"No, thanks, not at my age. Shep will see me out." He looked over the heads of the dancers at the ornate clock hanging on the far wall.

Joe laughed. "Come on, Bert. You're not that old!" He abruptly fell silent. "What's the matter? You don't seem yourself."

"Things are happening, Joe."

The only words he could find to explain. He leaned his head against the wall and compulsively rubbed his fingers together. "I don't like it at all."

Joe nodded, serious now. "You've seen that light in the sky? It's something bad coming, I reckon."

He paused for a moment. "I've been losing sheep. Three so far; the old weaned lambs. Can't be a fox, not when they're that size."

No, thought Bert. This was something far worse.

The music stopped and Joseph's voice rang loud in the silence. "My Alison reckons she heard a wolf howling last night. It came from over your way."

The world began to spin. Bert's chest tightened. He had to leave. He had to get back, now.

"I told her not to be ridiculous, but she's certain. Did you hear anything?"

Bert took a steadying breath. "No, I didn't."

Alison had been mistaken; of course she had. He'd have heard it else.

"Come on, Joe, come and dance!" Alison called from across the room.

Joseph looked at Bert, eyebrows raised. He nodded his acceptance and the pair inserted themselves into the crowd. Despite being well into her fifth pregnancy, Alison had managed to retain her figure and her verve for life. Not like his Janet. He felt a pang of envy as he hurried for the door before anyone else spoke to him. The bairn was laid wrong; that's what the woman had said. He'd only just had time to fetch the priest.

The past mingled with the future, and tears blurred his eyes.

14

As the door shut and the sounds of the dance faded, Bert thought he could hear muffled sobs. He hesitated, heard it again. He knew who it was, even before he rounded the corner of the inn.

Ellen was sitting on the step outside the Sunday school, her red hair curtaining her face as she leaned her head on her knees.

His boot caught a stone and she jerked upright. Shock, panic, recognition, then despair spread across her face.

"Uncle . . ."

She rubbed at her face, trying to disguise her tears. Shep glanced up at Bert and then went to her side, pushing his nose under her arm. She bent down and hugged him, burying her face in his neck.

Bert sat next to her. She looked quickly at him and then down again. He saw a flicker of hope amid the despair. She was hoping he'd help her, understand her. Do something. Anything.

The babble of voices and music grew abruptly louder and then quieted as someone else left.

"You're in trouble, lass."

She turned to face him, her mouth falling open in surprise. He held her gaze as fresh tears began to flow. She groped for her handkerchief.

He felt for her, he really did. Who had she to turn to? Her step-mother, obviously not. Maud had taken her on as her duty when she'd married Eddie. The other gossip-loving young women, the same. Felton . . . He clenched his fists and looked away.

"Jack's a good man. He's just . . ." She swallowed as her words stuck in her throat. "He says he's too young. He loves me, he really does. He says he does."

He could see her bottom lip trembling.

"It's the money, how we'd manage. Whether the mine stays open. But I could take in sewing, we could keep a cow. I could make butter. We'd manage."

Her confidence was heartbreaking and Bert struggled to meet her eyes. He knew how stories like hers ended. He put his hand on her shoulder, squeezing the frail bones under the skin.

"It'll work out, lass. Don't worry."

His voice, filled with an assurance he didn't feel, drew a grateful smile. Ellen dabbed at her eyes again.

"Thank you, Uncle. I knew you wouldn't think bad of him, like everyone else does. Jack's a good man, really. You can see that, can't you? He'll come around. I know he will. It's just a big thing, you know?"

Bert made himself smile back. It cut through his face like glass as he struggled to hide his feelings. Of course Felton had no intention of marrying her. He'd told her the pretty words she'd wanted to hear, and now she was ruined. Damn the boy! He'd always looked out for her, and now he felt a father's anger toward the boy. If only he were a few years younger, he'd whip the skin from his backside for him.

Ellen was oblivious to his seething thoughts. "There's a house up on the bank; Mrs. Tipping's old place. There's room to keep a cow there. It'd be ideal for us."

He could hear the newfound confidence as she planned her future. Perhaps he should tell her the truth. Perhaps that would be kinder. He shouldn't have given her a hope that would soon be crushed. Her innocent faith was going to slowly slip away as her belly grew.

"It means so much to me, Uncle, that you're not ashamed or angry." She wiped the last tears away and stood up. "I'd better get home. Maud will be waiting."

Bert watched her disappear, then stood himself, his anguish heavy in his chest.

He crossed the marketplace and started on the road home. The puddles and ruts were glowing an icy silver under the meager moonlight. His boots slipped on the frozen smoothness despite his hobnails.

As he crossed the burn he noticed a figure standing in the shadows on the bridge, partly hidden by the wall. He hesitated for a second. Who'd be out here at this time of night? Poachers? Robbers?

Shep was alert, but he didn't seem hostile; Bert knew well the subtleties of his moods. And who'd want to rob an old man anyway? He carried on, then recognized the figure and smiled grimly.

Felton was oblivious to his approach, despite his hobnails and the clicking of Shep's claws. He was leaning on the wall, looking down into the water. Bert stopped right behind him.

"All right, lad?"

Felton jumped around, almost falling as he slipped on a frozen puddle, then slumped back against the wall.

"Mr. Allenston." He glanced quickly at him.

The boy was troubled, definitely. At least he could give him credit for that.

"She's a good girl, our Ellen."

Felton stared at the water. The silence stretched on.

"It's just . . . so soon." He took off his cap and twisted it. "I'm young. She's young."

Not too young to play the game, though. No sense of decency or responsibility. At least in his day they had the honor to see the girl well. He'd proposed to his Janet right away when she'd told him. He gripped his stick and felt Shep tense.

"I do love her. I've told her that. But marriage, I just can't do it. I want to do things, see the world. I thought of joining the army, going to India. See snakes and tigers. I'm going to be stuck here with nothing for the rest of my life."

"It's too late for that, boy. You've made your future now. If you love her, think of her. Ruined. Thanks to you. She deserves better—much better—than you, but for heaven knows what reason she loves you. *You.* And your life belongs with her now."

He was surprised to see Felton bite his lip, his cap squashed in his fists.

"I do love her. I want her, but . . ."

Was that tears in his eyes?

He took a deep breath. "I need to live my life." He pushed past and strode away.

Bert looked down into the water, flickering silver and black as the crescent moon shone through the trees. What would happen to the poor girl now?

He trudged on, turned up the hill toward home. He couldn't bear to shatter her girlish dreams, but soon, shatter they must.

His thoughts were disturbed by a low rumbling. Shep's hackles were raised, his entire body rigid as he stared up the road ahead of them.

15

Far below him, Bran could see the blaze of torches. Some were fixed around the village wall, others danced as the hunters sought the intruder.

Perhaps it's only a bear, he prayed as he leaped down the hill. Three years before, a bear had got inside the crumbling walls. It had been cornered, terrified, and killed four dogs and a hunter before falling under their spears.

Please let it be that.

He touched the raven amulet at his neck, his other hand gripping his staff as he approached the gates. They were always barred now, but he could see the silhouette of a small figure perched on top of the wall. Old enough to stand guard, but too young to dare take part in the hunt.

The brief snow flurry was blown onward and the moon reappeared. In the cold light he could clearly see the tension in the small muscles gripping her bow. It was Mintana, her fear obvious as she looked down into the maelstrom of noise and movement within.

He started to call out to her, but driven by some sixth sense, she turned and looked down. Utter relief spread across her face and she almost fell from the wall in her haste to get the gates open.

The aroma of smoke, animals, and damp earth was mixed with the metallic smell of blood. A strange, discordant hum seemed to echo around the settlement. Men were shouting somewhere out of sight, children were crying. A dog roared savagely, the sound abruptly cut short.

"It was here!" the girl blurted, trying to make herself heard. "We finished repairing the wall this afternoon; Gods alone know how it got in." She cringed and moved closer to him. He squeezed her shoulder briefly.

"Back on the wall. Stay there until it's safe."

She scrambled up the stones and crouched low. Then he turned to face the darkness within.

It was dark. Too dark. The moonlight had vanished as quickly as it came, but it was more than that.

Its presence had leached through the settlement, tainting the air with a writhing miasma. A thousand invisible tendrils crept toward him. He struggled not to recoil. He gripped his staff harder and moved forward, toward the turmoil.

Between two buildings, their eaves almost touching. He felt as if he were walking into emptiness. He had to touch one of the wattled walls to reassure himself, then chastised himself viciously.

The track between the dwelling houses and craft buildings. A glimmer of ambient light now betrayed his surroundings. The shouts were approaching from his right. The echoing hum was more powerful now.

A shadow in front of him. Emptiness, deeper than the surrounding night. He couldn't see it, couldn't hear it, but a terrible presence screamed past his inner senses. That sickening sound bored into his mind, pulsed through his entire being. It was emanating from the beast itself.

It vanished at once between the buildings. The sense of a swirling, poisonous void lingered.

Bran stared. His mouth was dry; he was gasping audibly. Frightened, he realized.

He touched his amulet and ran shaking fingers through his raven's feathers, feeling the strength of his totem. *You never have to face a battle you can't win,* he reminded himself. He drew a breath and felt the power he commanded, the power of the earth and the Gods. He could do this.

Running feet and a blaze of torchlight. Four men, spears and blades gripped in white-knuckled fists, looked at him. Three others struggled to hold their dogs. Fearn's monstrous black hunting dog fought at its restraint.

Bran concentrated on the darkness, aware of the snarling fangs beside him. He took no comfort from them.

The air clawed at him as he advanced. He could feel it creeping over his skin. The hunters followed. Fearn's dog lunged forward, almost pulling the hunter from his feet.

They reached the narrow drove way between the buildings and the outer wall. The shadow had seemed to go left, toward the holding area for the cattle. The juddering in the air was more intense from that direction.

Bran felt that way with his inner senses, but could find no sign of it. He closed his eyes and concentrated. Visualized his way through every building and walkway. Nothing, but not that *nothingness*. He turned right.

The drove way narrowed. The walls grew higher.

Trapped. No way out but to fight.

He pressed on. Sweat beaded on his face. The hunters were at his back, but this would not be their fight. He focused on the strength within himself as the air began to vibrate.

The corner of the outer wall. More torches from the right. Between them, something was repelling the blazing light. It pooled harmlessly on the ground around it.

The hunters stared. At least one dropped his torch and fled.

Bran forced himself to step forward. The sense of terror intensified as it echoed back and forth between the hunters and the beast.

It was feeding on their panic, he realized. He should tell them to go. But he knew what would happen the instant he turned his back.

He kept going forward. A needle-sharp pressure was driving him back. The sound howled around him until he longed to press his hands over his ears. The most primeval, most unnatural thing he'd ever encountered. On Earth, in the spirit world, in the deepest recesses of Annwfn. Three paces seemed to take a lifetime.

It was dissolving his senses, leaving nothing but quaking terror. He couldn't go any farther. His soul had reached its limit. He struggled, limply, as the last of his awareness slipped into the void.

There was something familiar about it, he thought from far away.

It sounded like . . .

Like the war-harps he hadn't heard for half a lifetime.

The strings were tuned to the soul, could induce panic, joy, peace, sleep, as the musician desired. Bran smiled.

He was Pennaeth of the Pridani, and the beast's tricks were no match for him.

He let the sound flow through him and around him. It flowed like oil along his raven's feathers and spilled harmlessly away. He regained control.

He drew himself up tall, felt the immense power of the Goddess, the *earth*, flowing up through his body and into his soul. He forced himself closer, inch by inch. He was almost near enough to touch it.

He had the unsettling feeling, as he gazed upon this *nothing*, that it walked on two legs. He had a sense of lightning-blue eyes, invisible to the eyes of his body, utterly terrifying to his soul. He was nearly there.

It exploded toward him. Somewhere, far away, he heard the roar of the dog. He stilled his soul and mind. Frozen and reflective, the shadow couldn't touch him. It locked itself around him. Sucked the air from his nightmare cocoon. He couldn't breathe.

He raised his rowan staff. It was heavy as a grown man. His arms shook as he forced it chest high.

He felt the sacred sigils carved beneath his fingers. Of the Goddess, the One. With her son, as One became Two. Of her triple aspect as One became Three. And of the totality as All became One. His was the most powerful talisman known, worth a thousand spears and a thousand fangs.

Pain screamed through him as the cysgod-cerddwr forced his magic back. His hands grew slick with sweat. The wood slipped under his grip. The nightmare pressed closer. He was suffocating.

He fought for the power he knew was there. Beneath his feet. Between his hands. He had the Gods at his side. Sweat poured down his face and back. He threw his head back and roared as he locked his arms high. The force blasted through his feet, his arms, his staff.

He knew it was enough.

The beast was railing, crushed by his strength. It was beaten, he knew it.

And it knew he knew it.

He tried to force air into his chest. Sparks burst in his eyes.

The beast gave way.

The cysgod-cerddwr leaped for the outer wall. The seething blackness around him was gone.

Bran's knees buckled. He sagged onto his staff as air flooded into his lungs. Fearn's dog tore free and lunged. Its fangs snapped shut on empty air.

Bran was aware that his mouth was hanging open as he gasped painfully. Waves of dizziness flooded over him. The dog began to pace, snarling upward.

He began to shake. Apart from the dog and the frightened bleat of a calf, there was utter silence.

He slowly turned. Two dozen people were watching him. He opened his mouth but couldn't speak.

"He warned us." Fearn placed a trembling hand on his dog's head, both reassuring and for reassurance. The brute reluctantly lowered itself to his haunches.

"It came in the dark, but his barking woke everyone. We all lit torches and went out after it. It feared the light."

No it didn't. But Bran said nothing.

Fearn was glassy-eyed, almost speaking to himself. "If not for Twrch here." The fingers on the black fur entwined tighter.

The hunter had been truly frightened, Bran realized. He'd never known him afraid before.

"It was after the cattle?" Bran questioned, already knowing the answer.

Fearn shook his head. He turned and walked through the narrow gap between two buildings, pressing against his dog's shoulder. He didn't relax his grip on fur or leash.

Bran followed, some other men a few paces behind. He glanced back and saw the children held back by their elders.

The hunter stopped and raised his torch. The wattle of the building had been torn open. Through the gaping hole, framed by splintered laths and sagging thatch, Bran could see hastily abandoned sleeping furs. And blood. Fearn's cousin and his woman. She was with child, he knew.

The others crowded around, grim and angry.

"The spears did nothing. It was like they just hit a shadow." Bran recognized Coll's voice.

"My best iron blades! They've never failed before. They should have killed it."

Bran sought the smith's face in the crowd. It bore the expression of one whose beautiful illusion had been shattered. That everything he believed in was now worthless. He felt sorry for him.

Then he looked back at the bloodstained floor and felt shame and failure.

"But we frightened it away," someone said, desperate to believe.

Bran nodded. Let the man have solace in his hope.

In the distance he heard an answering howl, angry and terrible. Defeated. For now.

It would be back, and soon. He had a lot of work to do.

16

Bert scanned the road ahead, expecting a dog or a fox. Nothing.

"What is it, boy?"

Shep looked up at him, his eyes shining in the moonlight, and yapped. Then he went forward a few steps, looking up the hillside. Toward home.

There was a wolf out your way last night.

He became acutely aware of the icy wind tearing at his exposed skin. He began to hurry, desperate to see the silhouette of the stunted ash that marked the start of his own track. But it was nearly a quarter mile away yet.

Thick gray clouds were seething across the sky in the last glimmer of moonlight. The snow was earlier than he'd expected. Was that what Shep had sensed?

He knew it wasn't.

A flake of snow struck his cheek and melted, followed by another.

At last the ash tree materialized and he turned off the road. The snow intensified, a pale dusting which alighted for the merest second before vanishing. It wouldn't settle, not yet. The ground was too warm. It would be the early hours before that happened.

Head bowed, he struggled on, aware of nothing but the pounding blood in his ears, the sharp breath in his throat, the stabbing pain in his hip. He'd hurt it fifteen years ago slipping on a rock, and it still flared up in bad weather. But at least in the valley the wind was barely noticeable.

He reached the clump of rowans. Nearly there.

Another sound penetrated his mind. Shep was rumbling again, deep in his throat. He was looking toward the fold, to where he'd carefully shut his sheep earlier that evening.

Bert turned his eyes in that direction, squinting through the flurrying snow. He could already feel the tightness of dread in his chest.

The gate was smashed. Broken down by the sheer force of a hundred terrified animals. Shep slunk toward it, sniffed, then crept back.

Bert stared. Why had he shut them in? Dear God, he should have left them free. Free to escape.

He ran and fetched a lantern. Lit the wick with shaking hands and went to the fold.

What would he find? Blood, torn skin, entrails, ripped-out throats, clumps of wool. He could picture the scene only too well. Slowly, he forced himself to lift the lamp.

Nothing.

He allowed himself to close his eyes for a brief moment, then walked around the fold. He searched carefully with the lantern light. No blood, no torn wool. Nothing but the ruined gate suggested anything had happened.

So where were they?

He looked across the fell, his lantern throwing out a feeble orange circle that illuminated only flying snowflakes. Beyond was interminably stretching shadow. He closed his eyes and concentrated. He heard the soft whisper of the snow, the rasp of his own breathing, the pad of Shep's feet. Far away, toward Wooley, a dog barked. One of Scruffy Joe's, most likely. Three, four barks, then silence.

The quiet did nothing to calm his mind. The frantic blarting of sheep under attack would carry for miles, but they could be miles away by now.

He opened his eyes. Shep was looking dolefully up at him, his tail curled protectively beneath him.

"Where are they, boy? Find them!"

The dog whimpered and refused to move. Bert fought an urge to kick him. If his dog refused to find them, they were as good as lost.

But of course this beast was something entirely incomprehensible. He turned away and crouched down. There was no sign of fresh tracks, but then the ground was cold and hard, there was never likely to be. Where would they have gone? Where were they chased to?

He started forward on their usual trail toward the burn, and after fifty yards he crouched down again. Fresh dung. Shep sniffed along the track as well.

Bert straightened up. "Find them, boy!" he said again, hardly daring to hope.

The dog went off at a trot, heading toward the burn. Bert followed as best he could, lantern held high and using his crook for balance. It would be hard going to cross the slippery stones in the dark. He briefly saw himself falling, injuring an ankle maybe. But Shep went straight past the crossing point and up toward the fell gate. He darted left, heading toward the most desolate part of the fell. They began to climb.

Why had they come this way? They grazed here only rarely, mainly in spring when the heather was shooting. Surely they'd have gone somewhere more familiar?

Bert hesitated. Was the dog wrong?

"Where are they, Shep?"

The dog whined and looked back at him. He went a few steps farther, then looked back again. His message was clear. All Bert could do was trust him.

Eventually he had to pause to catch his breath. Shep stopped as well. The air was cooling fast and the snow was intensifying.

He pulled the hem of his jacket over his mouth to try and ease the daggers in his throat. The wind was rising now that they were on higher ground. It was ripping through the heather and driving snowflakes into his face and eyes. He took a deep breath.

"Ho! Ho!" he cried as loud as he could.

The sound carried across the moor and echoed back. *Ho! Ho!*

He stood motionless and listened. No answer except the wind. The pair struggled on across the spongy peat. Bert stumbled as his foot sunk deep into a boggy hole. He dragged himself free, his boot now soaking wet. There were no real treacherous bogs on this part of the fell, at least.

"Ho! Ho!" he shouted again.

They reached level ground, but the respite was tempered by the savage gale, which, now unchecked, tore at his jacket and numbed his fingers. The snow was already settling up here. Soon the tracks would be obscured.

He blew out the lantern and stuffed it into his pocket. It was all but useless anyway. Better he let his eyes grow accustomed to the dark. He could use his free hand now to hold his jacket shut. He tried to turn his collar up against the burrowing snow but the wind just whipped it open again.

"Ho! Ho!" he shouted again, the sound splintering in his frozen throat.

Shep stiffened midstride, his ears pricked. Then Bert heard it, too. Very faintly, carried by the wind.

"Ho!" he bellowed, relief strengthening his voice.

One, two, three, voices answered him. Bless you, Shep! He should have known he'd be right.

He began to trot after the dog, as fast as he dared, his footsteps loud on the deepening snow.

They rounded an incline and there was the valley by Hunter's Ford, a deep gouge in the hillside, dangerously sheltered from the prevailing winds. Once, when he was newly married, his sheep had come here to shelter from a sudden snow storm. It had drifted across the mouth and three had perished before he could dig them out.

He shouted again as he reached the lee of the hill, and there they were, his dear, faithful Molly at the front. She looked toward him and chortled deep in her throat. *I knew you'd come.*

"Ho! Come on, girls!"

They moved slowly, worried and nervous. What had happened, he had no idea. But somehow—perhaps when the snow began to fall—Molly had eventually led them here to safety. It could be a year since she last came here, but the memory of sheep was long.

He scanned over them. At least the rapidly whitening landscape made it easier to see. A few of them looked back into the valley and flicked their ears. They were upset, and not just by the snow. But they were all sound. All alert. There was none of the labored breathing or heaving flanks that would signify injury or distress. Whatever had scared them, thank the Lord it hadn't managed to harm them.

When he turned back, the snow had already drifted across the mouth, obscuring the heather plants. They had to hurry. Whistling to Shep, he turned and strode back toward home, knowing they would follow.

Shep knew exactly what to do. He ran behind the group and harried them on, keeping them tightly together as they reluctantly picked their way across the now invisible trail.

They passed one of the ancient boundary stones that ran across the fell, and Bert felt a flood of relief. Nearly there. Nearly home. They reached the lower ground where the snow was barely yet settling, and then they were off the fell.

The sheep balked for a moment when they reached the fold, but the snow had smoothed away any lingering traces of what had been there, and a few yips from Shep persuaded them to enter.

Bert dragged some hurdles across the gateway and tied them in place. Icy fingers of snow crept down his neck and melted as he watched them settle, then he retreated inside, uneasily satisfied that there was nothing more he could do. Whatever had been there, all he could do was hope it was far away by now.

17

It was gone. Bert was confident of that.

The sheep had been quiet in the night—he'd barely dared sleep, and Shep had lain on his rug with his ears cocked—so he knew he'd find all well. He pushed at the door but couldn't shift it.

"Well, Shep, I reckon it's come down a bit thick."

The dog's tail swept a semicircle on the floor.

Bert put his shoulder to the door and budged it a few inches, and then a few more, until there was just enough room to squeeze out. True to promise, it was over eight inches deep.

Sinking up to his shins, he went out into the sparkling, deafeningly silent world and smiled. It was the most beautiful sight. The rowan tree guarding the southern wall of his home looked stunning, each red berry topped with a tiny cap of creamy snow. Janet had planted it just after they were wed. Rowan was her favorite tree.

"You'd love this, Jan," he murmured, lightly touching the tiny ice crystals.

He pictured her, tugging his arm to come and marvel at it. He would chuckle indulgently and run his arm around her waist, pulling her close for a kiss. She'd twist away, teasing, and point out yet another wonder.

A tiny flurry of snow speckled his hand, and forty years came between himself and his memories.

"Imagine we'd grown old together," he said to himself, watching the snowflakes melt and vanish into the cracks of his fingers.

It was growing too big now, the roots would undermine the walls. He should have cut it down years ago, but couldn't bring himself to do it.

He took a shovel and began to clear a path to the fold. Dig, pitch, dig, pitch. It was nothing compared to the summers he spent loading hay wagons down the valley. He was barely sweating when he reached the fold.

The dark green ovals among the white indicated where each sheep had lain for the night. He watched as one, and then another and another braced themselves and shook violently, the balled snow flying from their fleeces. In the silence it sounded like a continuous rumble of thunder.

He opened the makeshift gate and the more adventurous were quickly outside, Molly in the lead. They began to expertly burrow through the snow to reach the grass. The younger ones, unfamiliar with snow, remained in a bemused huddle.

Bert looked across the valley at the higher fells around Acton Moor. Uniform blankness except for the piebald columns of the old smelting chimneys, which had snow blown against one side. It had fallen much deeper up there.

He'd have to wait a while before he could go back into town. The snow would have drifted high on the road, between its narrow walls. Around a week to melt, he estimated. The sun still lent some warmth. Snow in November, clear in hours; snow at Christmas, clear at Candlemas, so the saying went.

He leaned on his shovel. His wood store was full. Plenty of hay in the barn. He had a side of bacon hanging by his fireplace; several boilings of potatoes from his plot; plenty of apples; a sack of oats; a pork pie from Ellen. He was always well stocked. It was a good time to start the winter tasks. He had to make new hurdles, and he had some carving projects in mind as well. He was going to make Thomas a crook as a Christmas gift. *With a grouse's head,* he thought. The boy had been fascinated by their gurgling cry when he was younger, forever pestering Bert to take him up the fell to see them.

He'd be twelve soon, leaving school. Coming to live with him, following the tradition of generations. Bert was looking forward to it. He saw himself pointing out the deep sheltered gorges on Eshells Moor, where a ewe always seemed to hide her lambs. The two springs that could always be relied on in the driest summers. The spots where tormentil grew, the roots of which would cure diarrhea in the lambs.

There'd be room for a bed near the stove. A bit cramped, but warm. His boyish dreams of steam trains—Bert couldn't help but grimace—would fade, of course. His future was written in his blood. And when he was older and wanted to marry, perhaps they could build a new place for him nearby.

A twinge in his hip reminded him, he wasn't as young as he was. Perhaps there'd be no need for that.

His smile died away. He became aware, with an aching sense of loss, of the inexorable marching of time and change, sweeping him and all he knew aside, tossed about like fallen leaves on a mountain stream.

He remembered the words etched on the sundial on the church. "*Hora fugit,*" Thomas had carefully read once. "What does that mean?"

He'd no idea, but Thomas had bounced out of Sunday school several weeks later and told him: "It means, 'the hour marches on,' Grandpa!"

How true that was.

He looked across at the Fist, almost entirely obscured. At the clump of rowans, at the tiny gray houses down in the valley, bowed under their blanket of snow. At the faint speck of a kite interrupting the perfect blue sky.

How long would it last? Would he ever see such a dazzling vision again?

The sense of mortality grew more palpable. Would Thomas really continue after him? However much he hoped so, he couldn't help but doubt. The wind crept under his collar and he realized his foot was growing damp. The snow had soaked through his split boot.

He was spending far too much time thinking, he chastised himself. There was work to be done.

He started to wade through the snow, looking for any sign of the beast. He didn't really hope to find anything, but he needed to be doing something.

Shep bounded alongside him, powdered in snow, tail high, propelling himself into the air to clear the never-ending obstacle. Bert couldn't help but laugh.

After twenty minutes of careful and fruitless search, his mood had dissipated. The snow would have obscured all signs of the attack. If there had ever been any. It would be impossible to track. When one met it, it was only ever on its own terms. His grandfather had emphasized that time and again.

Hopefully it would back off now. It couldn't travel through the snow without leaving tracks, after all. Perhaps they'd be safe for most of the winter. He could leave dealing with it until the spring.

He nodded to himself. He was sure he was right.

18

Gleaming, sunny days followed silent, starry nights. The snow lessened. Bert and his sheep were left in uneasy peace. The only sounds were the dripping from the eaves, the occasional rumble of a tiny avalanche, and the persistent snuffling of burrowing sheep. The eerie light in the sky dimmed, visible now only on the western horizon after sunset.

His first task each morning was to spread the hay on the trampled snow, watch the sheep eagerly devour it, then fill two buckets with snow to melt. Normally he fetched water from the spring two hundred yards away, but now it was on his doorstep. Every cloud . . ., as they said.

He saw a robin hopping mournfully across the snow. It spotted a black speck and darted for it.

"You're getting hungry," he said.

When the buckets were warming he scraped up the crumbs from his rather stale loaf and scattered them on the snow. The robin was soon greedily pecking them up. When the snow was clean except for a scattering of tiny footprints, the bird looked at him, cocked its tail as if in thanks, and flitted away. Bert raised his hand in farewell.

He kept glancing down the obscured track, expectant of Thomas's approach and hoping he wouldn't be so foolhardy. It was a treacherous route in deep snow, and he didn't know the ground well enough. He'd have to show him how to make snow skates. They used to race on the hills with them when he was a boy. Just thin lengths of wood strapped to the feet, the difference they made was incredible.

It was time to start the boy's crook, he decided with a thrill. He took the horn he'd chosen, a beautiful piece from a five-year Swaledale ram. He'd traded one of his finest crooks for it at Hexham mart and used it for his most important projects.

He held it this way and that, studying its natural grain and contours until he could visualize the grouse's head locked within it. He hefted his knife in his hand and curled the first strip away.

His hand soon began to tremble. He hadn't carved anything like this for a few years, and it shocked him to realize how much his dexterity had declined. He put his knife down when the rough outline was formed and flexed his aching fingers. He winced as a sharp pain shot through his hand.

He stared at the shelf on the wall, barely able to focus on the array of bottles and earthen jars. A jar of tea leaves, one of raspberry jam. Cough cure. A cloth-wrapped piece of hard cheese. With an effort he got them into focus. Good thing he didn't do this too often any more. Last thing he wanted was his eyesight failing. A shepherd who couldn't spot the lone lamb a half mile away in the heather, who couldn't see the dart of a dropping raven, he'd be in the poorhouse in no time.

His gaze drifted to the flames for a while, then he picked up his knife again. It was probably straining his eyes, trying to distinguish the contours from the dancing shadows in this dim light. But carving had to be a nighttime task. He had too many other things for the daylight hours.

He persevered for three evenings. The bird was emerging from its confinement. The head and nape flowed out of the horn. Then it emerged up to its breast. He could see the eyes blink as the shadows drifted across it.

He'd been working for three hours this evening, he estimated, although he'd have to go and check the position of the Plough to be sure. Shep was snoring at his feet, his paws twitching as if chasing an imaginary hare.

He tried to lay the knife down but his fingers wouldn't unlock. Perhaps he should finish it. He couldn't wait for that feeling of intense satisfaction at a hard job well done. There were just the final touches to the face and beak. He focused again and began to make the final strokes.

Shep jerked awake and sat bolt upright. Bert jumped, and his hand slipped. A tiny chunk of horn fell to his lap. He gasped in horror. He couldn't believe what he was seeing. It was spoiled, ruined.

Shep, you damned stupid dog! he wanted to shout.

Shep was already creeping into the corner, his ears down. He knew he'd done something wrong. He whined, peeping at him with his head hung low.

"Not your fault," he said. The dog wagged feebly.

He looked at his masterpiece again. The beak hung low and lopsided, the beautiful symmetry shattered. He hurled it at the wall. Shep cringed lower.

He'd have to start again. It had to be perfect. It had to last Thomas his lifetime. When the boy was struggling to lever his aching legs over the rocks and streams as he taught his own grandsons the ways of the hills, he would be using it to steady his steps. His grandsons would ask him about the grouse head, and he could recount with misty fondness his early years on the fell.

Bert picked up his last remaining piece of horn, but he couldn't face starting again. Not now.

But he had to do something. He picked up a few odds of ash wood and began to whittle a galloping horse. Ellen's half-sisters always enjoyed his animals, as did Thomas's younger sisters.

He rasped at his creation with a piece of sandstone to polish it. It looked good; the girls would love it.

He stretched out toward the fire. He had plenty of time to redo the grouse. He'd done it once—almost—and he could do it again. After he'd carved a dog, staring acutely into the distance as Shep was wont to do, a couple of sheep, and a porker pig for Christmas gifts, he began the grouse again.

At last he fixed the head to the shaft and painted it, swirling the brown and black to resemble the mottled feathers of the hen grouse. The eyes and beak colored, the stick was finished.

He squinted at it and let his imagination take over. In his mind the bird turned to look at him, bent her head down to pluck at her breast. Shook herself to fluff up her feathers, which pulsed in the dancing firelight.

He opened his eyes fully and the carving returned to its original form. His grandfather had told him this was the only way to know if he'd captured the creature's form exactly. More than a mere carving, it was the mirror image of a soul.

19

He couldn't destroy it. That was now horribly clear to Bran. It had cost him dear just to force it from the village.

He shook his head, the memory still raw. He was one of the most powerful Druids in the land, and he'd gained the upper hand by the merest fraction.

It would have to be returned to its own world. Forced back the way it had come, through the portal of the otherworld. It was the only thing he could do.

He looked down on the village below, slowly emerging into the dawn light. Like him, everyone would be maintaining an uneasy vigil for sunrise. He could make out the hazy swirl of rising smoke, hear the cattle as they began to rouse themselves.

The eastern sky gradually turned a rich blue and Bran resumed his pacing of the hillside. Was it really the same night he'd begun debating the problem? He looked up at the last stars to hold out against the dawn. The Fiery Star was still there, now hanging low in the south, about to vanish behind the far hillside. Even as he watched, it began to grow dim.

He looked a moment longer, then dropped his head to his chest, his gaze lost among his raven's feathers, which danced and shimmered in the early morning breeze.

He needed the answer. Quickly.

When Samhain came and the otherworld portal reopened, he could lure the beast to the entrance. The ring of standing stones to the north, not yet emerged from the shadows. And if—*if*—with all his skill, he could hold it there until the portal closed at sunrise, the beast would be removed forever.

How to lure it?

His mind flickered back to the torn and savaged bodies in the village, a dark and fleeting notion, but the thought was abhorrent to him.

And Samhain was still nearly ten moons away. Far too long.

He paused abruptly. A cold thrill ran down his spine. A blast of wind whipped through his cloak but he paid it no heed as his mind began to whirl.

There was something he'd been told of, long ago. A way to imprison a soul, so tightly it could never again escape. He'd never heard of any Druid attempting it, and not without reason. It was the most difficult ritual known; more likely to end in death than success.

The beast would fight, of course. Resist to its utmost. He would need all the strength and wisdom he possessed, the collective experience of countless generations of Druids, and then he might have a chance.

His heart rate quickened. Would he be able to do it? Would he survive?

He knew, with a cold, calm certainty, that he *could*. That, of course, was why he'd been chosen for the task.

But it would not be easy. There was no guarantee that he *would* succeed.

He allowed himself a brief moment of pride that it was he who was to do it. The tale would be handed down in Druid lore forever.

He sat cross-legged on the grass and leaned back against the stone wall of his lodge. Stone, the symbol of death. Grass, the life force for hunters and prey. Day merged with night and night merged with day, a crossroads from which Bran could choose his path.

He ran his fingers through the frosty stems, feeling ice particles melt against his skin. He could feel the life singing through the hillside, and then the air was filled with sound. In the silence, the song of life was radiant. He let it fill him, speak to him. He emptied his mind and the song took on words.

It was one of the Histories, a tale he'd sung a hundred times to gatherings large and small.

Balor was the most ferocious of the Fomorii warriors. As a boy, he peeped into a sorcerer's forge, and the eddying smoke had poisoned his eye. From then on, the gaze of that eye meant death.

The Fomorii allowed him to live, on condition his eye was kept shut. It was opened only on the battlefields.

The Pridani's final battle with the Fomorii. Screams and slashing iron. A red mist cloaked the plain. Catastrophic slaughter, unimagined for either side.

Balor was brought forth. His eye was levered open.

Lugh, the Pridani champion, charged through the ranks. The poison was seeping toward him. He flung his javelin.

Balor's eye was driven straight through his skull. He fell down dead, and his eye fell among the Fomorii ranks, slaying thrice nine warriors.

Then the Pridani victory was easy.

It was a Druid from across the Western Sea, whom Bran had met on his years as a Wanderer, who'd told him the secret that only a few now remembered.

The eyes were the doorway to the soul. Using the sorcerer's spell he'd unwittingly stolen, Balor could bind another's soul to himself. Imprison it, breaking the bonds between its body, which gave it life.

But in doing so, his own soul became bound. Day and night, life and death. Harmony needed opposites. And Lugh—Druid trained, they all agreed on that—had shattered this prison of souls with Balor's own magic.

No Druid had ever attempted the same sorcery. To complete it, without losing one's own soul, had been discussed, debated, but never achieved.

Could he do it? He'd heard three dozen ideas. Formulated another half dozen of his own. Would any of them work?

As the light strengthened and the village emerged into the day, he saw his hare and red deer hind illuminated above the gate. Another thought came to him.

Artwork was an image of the soul. The Druids understood that; the Fomorii had not.

What if he created an image so perfect, the cysgod-cerddwr would recognize it as itself?

Warmth bathed the back of his neck and he turned to see the first glowing rays emerge. The night was over. Day was reborn. He knew what he was going to do.

20

When the Fist emerged from its wintry blanket, Bert knew the trail would be passable. Smatterings of shrubby green were breaking through the white as the heather emerged. Eight days since it had fallen.

He watched a kite soar across the fell and dive down on some prey—a vole, most likely—that had ventured above ground. It was a hard time for the raptors, with their prey snugly cocooned below the snow.

The bird glided up and alighted on the Fist, the knuckle of the first finger, glared around for competition and began to tear at its meager prize.

He remembered a story he'd heard when he was a bairn. A long-ago witch had buried a giant under the hill to stop him terrorizing the village. He'd tried to escape—and nearly succeeded—thrusting his fist out from beneath the rubble in his bid for freedom. The witch had to turn him to stone before any more of his body emerged.

He wondered if anyone else remembered the tale now. He'd have to tell Thomas and the other little ones. He loved telling the old stories as much as they loved hearing them.

He could see Molly poking into a thick bramble bush among the trees down the valley, a peculiar variety to which the leaves clung well into winter. He knew it would be her.

He leaned on his crook to watch. It always amazed him, the infinite delicacy with which they managed to pick the leaves off the viciously thorny plant. He could barely manage a half dozen blackberries without getting a thorn in his finger.

She backed out from the bush, disturbing a fluttering of snow as the thorns snagged on her wool. She looked toward three younger ewes, two-year-olds by the look of them, who were watching her enviously, and chortled. *Your turn.* All three raced to the bush, jostling to get the best spot.

Bert laughed and shook his head. They were an endless source of entertainment. How anyone could wish for a different life than this, he couldn't imagine.

He looked at the sun. Midmorning already. He'd have to go into town now.

What had happened, or not happened, in the last week? Was Ellen still expecting wedding bells? Did everyone know by now?

He'd have to tell her. He couldn't bear to, but it was for the best. He whistled to Shep and set off, rehearsing what he would say.

It was about a mile to the house where Maud now lived with her charges. The snow was rapidly melting, a dirty slush that dribbled into the ditches. Here and there he could see the marks of a homemade sledge. A flock of blue tits scurried through the bare trees, chirping incessantly as they searched every twig and crevice. They'd have been suffering the past few days.

Shep woofed and Bert saw Hilda Pinkerley, the butcher's wife, picking her way across the Philip Burn Bridge, holding her skirts out of the slush.

"'Morning, Bertram! Glad it's clearing at last!"

"'Morning, Hilda. How's things?"

"Not much trade, thanks to the snow. Just a few screwy rabbits our Micky's caught. He can't get near the mine these days. Sooner they get this big new road built, the better, I say."

"They've done more than enough damage in my view."

His words came out harsher than intended. Hilda glanced at him.

"Perhaps you're right. I remember my grandma telling me about when they built the New Road. One of those Irish laborers climbed down someone's chimney trying to rob them, only he got stuck. They found him when the fire started smoking. Everyone started fixing scythe blades across their fireplaces after that."

Bert chuckled. "I remember that one. Before I was born, that was. No wonder we've had no more roads since."

"You could get one built up to your place, make it easier for you. Our Micky said he saw you coming down through the snow."

Bert studied Hilda's face. There was no smugness or tiny smile to indicate a juicy secret she couldn't possibly divulge, not unless pressed and cajoled of course, until she was reluctantly drawn to confide it. Hilda Pinkerley was the biggest gossip in town, noisy as a pair of kestrels, and if she didn't know, it was pretty sure no one did.

"You'll be calling on young Ellen, no doubt?"

He nodded. Was that a smile on her lips?

"You'd best get on, then."

There was definitely a sly smile there. Had he been wrong? He felt a deep gnaw of dread in his chest.

He hesitated as he reached the cottage, then thumped on the door.

"Ah, Bertram. I was expecting you half an hour ago. The delivery boy said you were coming."

"Er . . ."

He looked at Maud. Why wasn't she at work?

"Leave that animal outside, please."

He looked down at Shep. Ellen always allowed him inside. Then he realized why Maud was at home. Of course, too shamed to go out. Perhaps even lost her position.

He gestured and Shep sat down on the cobblestones, meeting his eyes with a sorrowful gaze as he stepped inside.

Ellen was sewing on the settle. Bert's prepared words vanished, and he braced himself for her tears.

She jumped to her feet, a smile breaking over her face. "Uncle! I'm so glad to see you!"

He tried to mask his surprise. Whatever Hilda Pinkerley thought she knew, it wasn't that. "You look on cloud nine, lass."

"I'm to be married!"

He didn't know what to say. Questions buzzed through his mind.

"Jack asked me last week. It's to be next month, before Christmas."

He found his voice at last. "Congratulations, lass! That's champion news!"

He hoped it would turn out to be true.

He heard muffled giggling. The girls were perched on stools in a corner, their hands clapped over their mouths. He'd not even seen them.

"Catherine! Heidi! Be quiet!" Maud snapped. The girls subsided into guilty silence.

"It is time you were settled down, my girl. Although how we'll manage, I don't know. At least the Fairlies are abroad this month and not next, else I wouldn't afford a scrap of bread."

There was an awkward silence. Ellen's sewing went a long way toward their living. Bert groped in his pocket and waved the wooden toys he'd carved for the girls.

Ellen's face was full of womanly confidence. "Jack's been to see about Mrs. Tipping's house; he thinks it's perfect, too."

She jerked her foot back as Heidi's pony vaulted it. The girl scrabbled across the floor between them. There was a squeal and a clunk from near the settle.

"Girls! Go outside and play if you can't behave yourselves!"

The children got up and sidled from the cottage. Ellen looked down and fiddled with her dress.

"Would you . . ." She glanced up again. "Would you give me away, Uncle?"

He couldn't speak. He gazed at her hopeful, nervous face. The proudest moment a man could have, and one he thought life had denied him.

"I'd love to, lass."

She flung her arms around him and hugged him, her hair soft against his stubble. "I'm so glad."

He held her for a long moment and hoped that all would turn out right, that Felton wouldn't break her heart.

At last she stepped back. Her face clouded.

"Other things have been happening, since the snows came."

"What do you mean?"

In an instant he knew.

"People have been losing sheep. Cousin Joseph, he lost some lambs awhile ago."

"I know. I spoke to him at the dance."

"It's got a lot worse since then. Three or four more people have had problems. Samuel Gatesby's one of them."

In the valleys. Less snow, a degree warmer, much easier to move without leaving a trail.

"All lambs again?" He chewed his thumbnail.

"No, adult ewes now. Two or three a night. Nothing left but the skins and horns, sometimes a chewed bone. The men have hardly dared sleep. They keep their guns ready, their dogs loose, but it keeps happening."

He had to sit down. He realized with a sick feeling what a mistake he'd made.

The cottage door opened and Kate ran in, pigtails flying. "Mom! Ellen! There's been another one!"

"What, Catherine?"

"Mr. Gatesby, two of his sheep were killed last night! Bobby Laxton just told me. They've just found them by the Scar!"

Bert levered himself up. "I'll have to go and see."

It'd be a terrible blow. Samuel had been stricken with sickness during the summer and lost a score of animals.

"Can I come, too?" Kate looked up at him eagerly.

"No, Catherine. It's no place for children."

"Mam!"

"Catherine! No!"

"Come here, Kate. You can help me unpick this stitching." Ellen patted the settle and picked up her work again. Bert hurried from the cottage.

The crowd was swelling in front of him. He elbowed his way to where Samuel was staring into the air. Did people have nothing better to do than gawk?

He saw Mick Pinkerley. His face was a mask of horror, fear, and something else. Guilt. The boy turned and saw him. His expression was like he'd been caught with his fingers in the apple store.

"Mr. Allenston . . ."

Somebody knocked the boy off balance. He lurched forward and trod on Bert's foot. He muttered an impatient curse and pushed past him.

Then he saw it. He stopped and stared, and an icy feeling crept over him. He realized exactly what he was facing.

21

The first thing Bran had to do was to find the beast. When he had done that, he could begin the process of imprisoning it. The hunters had failed utterly to locate it, but there were other methods he could use.

He hurried back to his lodge and ducked behind the drapes. The thick, smoky atmosphere struck him forcibly after his night in the chill open air. The peat he'd banked the fire with at sunset—what seemed a lifetime ago now—had smoldered to nothing but the air had barely cooled. Not like the feeble buildings of the invaders. They apparently came from a warm and sultry land; they had no idea how to live comfortably in the lands of the Pridani.

Bran tied the drapes shut, stirred the fire to expose the embers, then built it high with dry wood. It was soon blazing, and the room was bright with dancing light and shadow.

He sought out a bowl and his grinding stone, then untied a leather sack hanging from the roof. He took out two pouches, one containing the dried stems of the red spotted mushroom, and the other the dried berry of the nightshade. Together they would free his soul from his body, so his spirit could search for the soul of the beast.

He tipped some of each into his hand, studied it, then added a pinch more nightshade. Too little and it would be useless. Too much, the fragile link between body and soul would break and he would not be able to return. He tipped the plants into the bowl, added water and honey, and began to grind the concoction to a fine paste.

The potion ready, he sat cross-legged in front of his fire, looking into the flames as he slowly sipped it. His mind and stomach rebelled at the vile taste, and he had to force himself to swallow. In a few moments the cup was empty. Already he could feel the plants' magic spreading through his body. The strange sensation as it began to prize his soul free.

The flames were mesmerizing. He could feel them dancing around his body, in front of his eyes, even when he turned his head away. He was much more light-headed than normal. Had he made it too strong? The thought spun out of his mind as the swirling flames took over again.

He lay down flat. The movement made him feel as if he were spinning hands over feet, like that cartwheel game the children played. His skin was cold and clammy. Like he was lying in an icy puddle. He tried to turn his head to see if he was. He saw his body lying on the floor beside him.

He was looking old, he thought dispassionately. When had his hair grayed so much? Then he began to rise and slipped through the smoke hole in the roof.

He swooped and soared, flapping his wings experimentally as he grew accustomed to the strange sensation. His glossy black feathers hummed as they carved a path through the air. He reveled in his freedom, watching the rainbows dancing across his wings in the sunlight.

He fixed his gaze on an inviting bare branch high in a pine tree and swooped toward it. The air whistled past him as he plummeted, faster and faster. He carefully adjusted his wing position, then outstretched his talons in readiness.

He folded his wings at what he judged the correct moment, but it was a little too late and he almost went tail-over-beak. He flicked his wings down flat and spread his tail feathers for balance. His claws gripped deep into the bark as hard as he could, and he at last felt secure enough to look down without losing his balance.

He could see a deer nibbling tree bark a hundred paces away. Cattle wandered, grazing what meager grass they could find. Farther up the fell, the small black dots of sheep ranged about.

He heard human voices and looked down through the branches. Fearn was approaching with some of the youngsters, all carrying their bows and quivers.

"Three apples," he was saying, "to whoever can hit the target at a hundred paces."

Bran saw the exchanged looks of excitement. The group passed beneath him and he carefully stepped around on his branch so he could follow their progress.

Fearn suddenly glanced back, and their eyes met for a moment. Bran saw the hunter's grip tighten on his bow. He braced himself to swoop away, but the hunter merely nodded slightly and continued after his pupils.

Bran opened his beak and dipped his head down in relief. Fearn had never been schooled by the Druids, despite his very obvious natural ability. He'd preferred to remain focused on his one true passion.

What if he'd chosen otherwise? It would not be Bran as Pennaeth now. The sobering thought focused his mind.

He shut his eyes and saw the landscape in a new form, one of swirling colors and shapes. The auras of life, seen through the eyes of the soul.

The people glowed a shimmering red, mingled with a rich blue. The arms of the first archer glowed as he prepared for his shot, then a bolt of energy flew through the air. It struck the ground and the color was absorbed into the earth.

He took in the trees, a deep rich green. The grass, shrubs, and rocks, the river and the sky. All pulsated with the heartbeat of life. With memory and destiny. He looked across the fell to where the sheep were now a soft, fleecy yellow. A red and blue shape watched over them, sitting in a natural rocky alcove that formed a wonderfully pleasant sun trap. He hadn't noticed the shepherd earlier.

Other sheep were being walked up the narrow drove lane that led to the fell near the Clenched Fist. The sheep snatched mouthfuls of grass as they hurried on.

He saw them all, then. Layer upon layer, shepherds and sheep, a thousand years past and a thousand years future. An eternal memory embedded between the ancient walls.

He turned again and began to feel across the land, seeking that void of blackness. He went farther and farther. The land passed through his mind as he sought through every crag, every cavity, every valley.

It wasn't there.

A surge of despair. Could it hide its soul as well as its body?

He had to find it. He traveled far toward the south. On the edge of his soul's limits, he felt the massive, concentrated, alien force of the invaders. He shuddered at the intense throb of energy, exuding colors he'd never seen before. A strange resonance probed inquisitively back at him. Don was right about their priests: they were powerful. He stored the thought away as he turned his awareness back to the north. The cysgod-cerddwr did not lie in the invaders' direction.

A long while later, far in the distance, a hint of blackness. He went closer. It grew bigger, more definite. A void of nothingness among the familiar colors of his land. He'd found it.

He opened his eyes and found himself in front of a cave, leading deep underground. He recognized the place; nearly a day's journey from the village, although the beast could cover the distance in, how long?

Nobody lived near this spot. Not even forage for a handful of sheep. He looked around but could see no physical sign of its presence. No bones, no tracks. He knew his raven's eyes wouldn't miss the slightest scrap of flesh. He cocked his head to one side

but could hear nothing. It could disguise its presence exception-
ally well, but thank the Gods it couldn't disguise its soul.

He hopped to the entrance, his wings outstretched slightly, but
he couldn't cross the threshold. Something was repelling him. He
flapped his wings hard, but to no avail. When he closed his eyes
again, his soul vision was overwhelmed by sudden, suffocating
blackness. He recoiled in shock.

A sharp tug at his back, and as he started to hop around he
found himself being hauled backward. He flapped his wings hard,
trying to fight the assault, but lost his balance. He was now beak
to the sky, his feathers snagging on sharp stones as he was hauled
painfully away from the cave.

22

A bloodstained skin. A shattered skull, one horn still attached. A thigh bone, splintered by an incredibly powerful jaw. Everything else was gone. Devoured. What had done this, Bert wondered, even though he was the only one who knew the answer.

He took a long breath and tried to look away. All that time he'd wasted, hoping—pretending—it wasn't happening. The ruined eye sockets bored accusingly into his face. This was his fault. He'd been entrusted with a task, and what had he done? Nothing.

Samuel Gatesby's face was grimly impassive, but his eyes betrayed him. There were tears in the eyes of his permanently cheerful cousin. "My two best ewes, Bert. I really needed them." He swallowed hard. "I'm ruined now. Ruined."

"I've got some good ewe lambs; I can sell you some." He could ill afford it, but he had to do something.

Samuel nodded absent thanks as Scruffy Joe joined them. He recoiled at the sight and the three men shared a long look. This was every shepherd's worst nightmare.

"It must be a monster of a dog, a real brute. Where's it coming from?" someone in the crowd asked. "Someone must have seen it or heard it."

"There were gypsies around in the autumn. They had dogs, didn't they?"

There was a murmur of disagreement. "They're long gone. And their dogs aren't capable of a thing like this! They're just for hunting hares."

"A wolf?"

"There are no wolves around here!"

"There are, though. My granddad, he saw one once when he was a lad."

"They're all long gone."

There was a moment of silence as Bert tried to order the turmoil in his mind.

"What about those people from near Haltwhistle? Moved here from away, a few years ago. They've got a house full of animals from foreign places. Lions, tigers, wolves, the lot."

Hilda Pinkerley had the crowd's full attention.

"Spent time in India in the army, he has. My niece works there as a housemaid, and she hates it there. All these strange servants, dark as the night and won't speak a word of English. Those animals howling through the night. Like as not, one of his wolves has escaped. That's what's done this." She nodded enthusiastically and smoothed her apron.

A murmur of relief ran through the crowd. But young Mick, Bert noticed, looked even more distraught.

"Shouldn't be allowed!"

"Disgrace!"

"It should be found and shot!"

"Perhaps we can track it?" Samuel asked without hope. "It was over your way last week, wasn't it, Bert? Is there any sign of a trail?"

Of course there isn't, he wanted to cry. "Unlikely, but no harm in looking."

"It's pointless," Joseph said. "There's no tracks, nothing. My dogs are frightened of it, whatever it is. They won't follow the scent."

"But we've got to do something. Where would it lair up, a wolf?"

Bert looked into the distance. A tiny movement flickered over a patch of snow. A stoat, most likely. A search, however futile, would be better than doing nothing. And he needed time and space to think. To work out what he should have done.

"There's that flue line past your way, Joe." Samuel gestured toward the chimneys up on the hill. "It's partly collapsed near the top—could be a good lair."

"Bit close to home, I'd think. How about the crags around Brownley Hill? There'd be plenty of places there for it to hole up."

"Aye. It's four miles, but probably nothing to a wolf. Can't think of anywhere else offhand."

The search was arranged. The three shepherds set off, heading for Wooley so Joseph could pick up his dogs and his guns. It was a nine-mile round-trip; no great hardship. Bert pushed the pace as hard as he could, both to punish himself and to get it over with. The rapid crunch of his boots on snow, ice, and frozen peat beat a rhythm in his head that drowned out his other senses. *Your fault your fault your fault.*

The excited barking that announced their arrival at Wooley was almost a surprise.

The two dogs were kept on long chains at the bottom of the track leading to Joseph's part of the fell, to deter any sheep who may get it in mind to wander. Guard dogs, watch dogs, alarm dogs. Attack dogs, if need be.

The brown-coated dog on the left went quiet as it recognized its master, but the second, a black, mangy-looking thing with walled eyes kept barking and lunging despite Joseph's shouts. Eventually a poke from his stick quieted it.

"Which one's had the pups you're trying to sell, Joe?" Samuel glanced at Bert and grinned with only a little shakiness.

"They're from old Meg. The missus has her in the house."

"Aye, but which one sired them?"

"Bloke I met at the market. Champion dog he's got. First class pups they'll make, worth every farthing."

The clatter of running boots announced another arrival. Thomas, and Joe's eldest—Hughie, Bert thought, although he could never quite remember—appeared in the yard, still in their school clothes.

"What are you two doing here?"

"We were let out early for dinner, and I brought Tom to see the pups so he can choose which one he wants." The boy paused. "We heard what happened, Dad. Can we come and help search?"

Samuel chuckled. Thomas looked at Bert for support. He gestured noncommittally and looked over at a wood pigeon plucking ivy berries fifty yards away and swallowing them whole.

"Well, seeing as you just happen to be here . . ."

Bert looked back to see Joe wink. The boy turned to Thomas with a fist raised in victory. Joe unclipped the dogs' chains and the black cur slunk forward.

"Thomas, no! Rip, get away!"

The black cur slunk back before crouching again. Thomas was on the cobblestones, his face contorted, rolling up his trouser leg. Blood was already dripping onto the ground. Hughie looked on in dismay.

"Thomas, how many times have I told you about him?" Joe was inspecting the wound.

Four puncture marks, nothing serious. Just a sore leg to teach him a lesson. Bert dug in his smock for the packet of yarrow he kept on him at all times. He tipped out a few fronds of the plant, spat on his palms and rubbed it into a green paste. He pressed it against the wound.

"Hold that there," he instructed. "It'll stop the bleeding."

Thomas winced as the juice stung the wounds. He stared up at him, searching for sympathy.

"It's your own fault, lad. Should take better care."

Thomas looked down but Bert could see the tears welling. Hughie looked like crying as well. Joseph went inside for his gun.

The bleeding stopped within a minute. Amazing stuff, yarrow. It could be a lifesaver when alone in the fells. Bert clicked his fingers to Shep as Joe reappeared.

"Let's get on. We've wasted enough time already." He didn't bother to see whether or not the boys were following.

The three shepherds set off up the hill, and a minute later the boys ran up beside them. Subdued, Thomas moving with an exaggerated limp, but otherwise all self-pity gone. None of the men acknowledged it. If Bert had got himself bitten at that age, neither his father nor his grandfather would have gone as far as giving him yarrow to stop his boot filling up with blood.

"Hare up yonder, look." Joseph pointed up the slope to their right. Bert picked it out at once. Pure white except for the eyes and nose, a perfect camouflage against its snowy backdrop.

"Where?" Thomas said at last. "I can't see anything."

Joseph pointed again. "That circle of heather then come left twenty yards to the rock, then down a bit to the middle of that snow patch."

"I've got it!" Hughie cried.

Thomas still looked blank. Bert was beginning to feel embarrassed.

"I can see it," Thomas said with relief as the hare began to move.

"I was thinking you needed glasses for a minute. Your grandpa can spot a flea on a dog's backside at fifty paces. You're letting the side down."

Thomas half smiled, unsure if that was a joke.

"Come on, we're not here for wildlife watching," said Samuel. "Let's crack on."

They soon reached the chimneys. Part of the old underground flue had collapsed, sealing the downward section with stone and turf. All eyes were drawn to the upper entrance. A narrow track of bare ground led into the tunnel, in glaring contrast to the rest of the ground, which was scattered with detritus and melting snow. Something was living inside. The pungent, musky odor told them what. As soon as Joseph waved the dogs inside, it made a bolt for safety.

"A fox, look!" Thomas cried.

It bounded across the snow, the dogs in swift pursuit.

"Back here! Now!" Joseph shouted.

The brown collie reluctantly gave up the chase. Rip developed sudden deafness for another fifty yards before ceding to Joe's increasingly furious holler. The fox zigzagged across the snow and vanished below the rise.

There was no point searching further—obviously the fox wouldn't share its lair with a wolf. They cut across the fell toward Brownley Hill, skirting the darker area of boggy ground to the left.

"Your granddad got stuck down there once, Hughie." Joe gestured as they climbed up to the crags. "A proper wet April, and he tripped jumping over a stream. Damn near drowned himself."

"Was he all right?"

"Clarted up with mud from head to toe, nearly wrenched his shoulder out, and your grandma was heard scolding him in town. Otherwise, bonny."

It was immediately obvious that nothing was living around the crags. Not even a footprint from a solitary grouse in the snow. The party soon turned back for home.

The low-lying sun still emitted some warmth, and Bert was sweating despite the chill air. The snow was rapidly melting wherever the sun fell on it. Over the tramping boots he could hear the *chu-chuck* of a grouse down in the valley, a gushing burn swelled by the snow melt, a skylark singing. The melody trickled down through the air and he squinted up to make out the tiny speck amid the blue.

The song of the fells washed the blackness from his thoughts, and the steady pace relaxed his body. Cursing himself once more for the time he'd wasted, he began to think what to do.

The first thing he needed was something to imprison the beast in. A likeness so good that its soul would be fooled into thinking it had found its way home.

He would have to use wood; that was where his talent lay. What it had been originally imprisoned in, he didn't know. All he knew was that something had enabled it to escape.

He began to visualize the wolf's head he would carve, running through every step of the process in his mind. He was confident he could do it. His grandfather had drilled him in every technique and trick he knew. He'd been renowned for his craftsmanship all through the district—he'd even made a pair of ptarmigan for his lordship's library—and Bert had inherited his talent. He'd only really seen it as a hobby before, but now he understood the true purpose of his schooling.

"Old Walter's place," he heard Joseph say.

He looked around. Ellen's grandfather—his uncle—had lived here. Several years abandoned, already the stone walls were crumbling and an ash sapling was growing in the doorway.

The girl had struggled up here almost every day, with a pie, a loaf of bread, a half dozen apples. She'd often brought things over to Bert as well, the start of their long friendship.

He thought back to that terrible day. She'd come running across the fell, her legs and dress spattered with mud, gasping sobs as she threw her arms around him. He'd got there as quick as he could but it was too late. They said later his heart had given out.

He stood lost in the past for a moment, staring at the ruined building that would never again home a shepherd. Was this to be the future? Was all they lived for, worked for, died for, destined to crumble under the grinding motion of time, reduced to nothing but dust and memories?

When he looked around he was alone apart from Joseph, who was watching him steadily. "All right, Bert?"

He took a deep shaking breath but couldn't answer.

23

Bran struggled to right himself but just ended up with a beak full of dirt. He tried to spit it out but his strange thin tongue couldn't dislodge it. He raked his claws out but they found no purchase on the loose gravel. He twisted his neck around but couldn't see any sign of his invisible attacker.

Then it dawned on him what was happening. Why hadn't he realized at once? Perhaps he had made the drink too strong, after all. It had been too long since he'd done this. The magic was wearing off. His soul, repelled by the danger ahead of it, was rushing back along the fraying spirit paths toward his body.

He relaxed and hurtled backward even faster. He managed to right himself and watched the cascade of sky and ground passing in a blur until he was sucked back through the smoke hole of his lodge.

He opened his eyes and saw the flames were now dimly glowing embers. He was cold and stiff and a dull ache nudged at his hip. But he knew where the cysgod-cerddwr was hiding.

Did it know he'd found it? That depended on how good its soul vision was. If it had seen him, it would move.

Or it would be waiting when he returned to the cave.

He pushed himself onto his elbow, blinking to clear his vision, and reached for more wood. He recoiled at the strange sensation of rough bark under his fingertips; he'd been half expecting to feel his claws still. He looked down his body to reassure himself.

The fire kindled into tiny flames and he huddled closer to it, tucking his cloak as tightly as he could around himself and drawing his numb feet close to the heat. When the soul was outside the body for even a short time, the flesh rapidly chilled like ashes in a hearth. That was why the soul was understood to be something akin to fire.

But then those with the fieriest souls—he thought of Coll—should therefore be the most powerful. The flames danced across his eyes as he thought about Coll, and Beth, and Beth's unborn child. An idea began to form in his mind, but as with the lingering effects of the potion, it refused to be pinned down.

There was a scrape on the door drape, which at once dispersed his fragmented thoughts.

"Come in," he called as he got himself up. To his disordered mind the sound was rather like the squawk of a raven.

He wasn't surprised to find Beth struggling to duck her unwieldy body through the door. Thoughts triggered events, and those events themselves triggered the thoughts that preceded them.

Beth hesitated as she took in his slumped posture and obvious chill, then her eyes went to the dregs of the drink, the contents immediately familiar to her. Her head twitched as she noticed the distinct aroma of the nightshade lingering in the heavy air. She gave him a quick smile of understanding and apology, then came farther into the room.

He tottered slightly as his numb feet betrayed him, then focused. He could see she wasn't ill, in pain or agitated. Rather, she seemed sad, weighed down and lethargic. As he looked at her, slightly off focus, he was aware of a dullness in her vital energy. Of course the loss of her son had devastated her, but something else was troubling her as well.

"What ails you, Beth?" He guided her to a stool against one of the roof poles.

She lowered herself down and leaned back gratefully against the timber, one hand supporting her belly, then stretched her feet out in front of her. Her ankles were swollen, he noted.

She pushed her limp hair back from her face and raised her eyes to him. He seated himself opposite on another stool, grateful he'd managed the maneuver without his body betraying him.

"I'm worried, Bran. Worried and frightened."

Her fingers plucked at a stray thread of wool on her cloak. "Ever since Raith died, I've been feeling, more and more, that all our past, all of our existence, is being swept away. I worry there'll be nothing left when this one reaches adulthood." Her hand compulsively stroked her belly.

Bran tried to gather his thoughts, threw more wood on the fire. He had to think carefully. She was right, of course, but he had to disguise that from her.

"You feel the same?"

He started and looked into her cool gray eyes. Curse that drink! It had befuddled his thoughts too much. Better she'd come when he'd had time to recover.

He chose his words carefully. "I saw the King Stag, wandering in his dying moments, not far from the Clenched Fist."

She nodded slowly. There was no need for him to explain further.

"Will we survive?"

"We will always survive. We are a part of the land, and the land will survive forever. We may not recognize or even like what we are to become, but we will still be here."

A finger of wind crept past the door drapes and swirled an eddy of smoke between Beth and himself, clouding and distorting Beth's face. For an instant he saw another face looking back at him, young but as old as the land, gentle but unconquerable, transient yet immortal. He shivered. The breeze stilled and the image was gone.

"My baby," she continued, her eyes carefully on his. "Coll is saying when he's born, he will become a great leader on account of his parentage. A Druid." She swallowed. "Pennaeth."

She waited for him to respond, her face expressionless. Although loyal to Coll, she was also loyal to her village and its people.

"I know what people will say, Beth. It will come to a challenge and battle for leadership. I know well what may happen, but no one can stop the future. It will be the way it's meant to be."

That was the truth, he thought. And the truth would test everyone's faith in the time to come.

"What will happen will strengthen us," he said calmly. "Who leads the Pridani into the future will be the best leader. And we need the best leader."

She smiled then, with sad, resigned acceptance. They both knew that individual lives were naught but the merest flicker, as transient as a leaping spark or a dying star in the sky. It was only when all were combined—into the eternity of the night sky, into the glowing flame of life—that their true value became manifest.

"Coll is adamant it is to be a boy."

She sat up straight, looked around the hut, then searched his face. "It's just a woman's feeling, I haven't said anything to him, but I wonder if it is to be a girl."

"I believe the same."

He saw the jolt in her body, the shock as her feeling was confirmed. Her mouth fell open slightly.

The babe had been conceived during the Beltane festival last spring. The smoke from the great fire, the symbol of rekindled fertility, had blanketed the celebrating crowd with a thick haze. But everyone had seen the shadowy figure appear. And they had all seen the horns rising from his head.

The shadow drifted through the crowd, entrancing all those present, including himself, and then took Beth by the hand and led her away into the night. What had happened, she'd never disclosed, but it was no surprise to find she was with child.

What would the future hold for the babe? The question had been pondered by all and voiced by a daring few. A child fathered by the Horned God himself, he would become a Druid surpassing all others. A warrior, a leader, a Pennaeth. An Arch Pennaeth.

And if it were a girl?

Only women could truly resonate with the ebb and flow of the Goddess. Only the female was the true vessel of life, the symbol of hope, of the future. That was why he'd carved the hind and not the stag as the village talisman. And this girl child, sired by the Horned God himself, would carry the inherent nature of both the Goddess and her Son, unite the Two into One. A phenomenal blend of spirit and strength.

And the timing could be no accident. The land would need this strength like never before.

Across the hazy room, their eyes conveyed all this without words.

Bran was the first to break the silence. "You're right to say nothing about it. It's a revelation that should be announced to the people as a whole; it will have great repercussions for everyone. I would be grateful if you would keep it to yourself for a while longer."

24

Bert would have to carve the head from hawthorn. The tree of the spirit world, standing sentinel at the doorways into the realm of shadows. All children were warned of the dangers of playing or falling asleep beneath it. The beast would be drawn to this familiar presence in a strange world, making his task so much easier. Now he had to find a suitable piece.

The tree emerged, ghost like, from the early morning mist. Bert shivered as he stood beneath the bare, cold branches, gnarled by nearly a century of growth. Only a handful of bright red berries remained, lending a meager splash of color to a bleak world.

A starling landed on the topmost branch with a screech, then hopped down to gobble a few berries. It eyed him accusingly for a second, then retreated farther up the branch.

He laid his hand on the thick roots, which twisted into the ground. The wood would be perfect. But somehow, it felt wrong to desecrate this ancient tree.

Use your intuition, his grandfather had said. *You will know when you have the right piece.*

Although this would be perfect—aged and mature, a dream to carve—it didn't feel right. He hesitated for a second.

He'd take it anyway. It was unlikely he'd find a better piece, and he didn't have the time to search farther.

He took out his mattock and laid the cold blade experimentally against the root.

He felt it shudder; he was sure he had. The starling took flight.

He lifted the mattock away and the mist silently breathed around him. Was that a sigh of relief he'd heard? He looked uneasily over his shoulder.

The indistinct forms of rocks, sedge, and heather swum in and out of the fog. The silence enshrouded him. Even the familiar presence of Shep was missing. This was a ritual he had to perform entirely alone.

Use your intuition.

With an impatient sigh he struggled to his feet. He carefully noted the position of the tree so he could return to it if necessary, then walked on.

He walked for most of the morning, examining every hawthorn that grew in the shelter of the long valley. None of them were suitable. He began to wonder if he would ever find what he was looking for. Maybe he'd been right the first time. That the first piece he'd found had been perfect; surely that wasn't a coincidence?

He looked back along the valley. He could barely see a hundred yards, and the tree was nearly four miles back. His trousers were clinging to his legs where the damp had soaked through them, the myriad tiny droplets that had formed on his hair had condensed to trickle down his neck, and the dampness of the grass was seeping into his cracked left boot.

Trust your instincts. What should he do? He stood there for a long moment.

A loud screech behind him and he turned. Perched on the path he'd been following, looking sideways at him with a glimmering eye, was a huge raven. The gleaming, midnight blackness of its feathers was a stark contrast to the gray dullness around it. He stared, transfixed.

The raven bent its head and began to preen at its wing feathers, never breaking eye contact. Then it hopped a few steps along the path, farther up the valley. With another loud caw, it spread its wings and merged into the fog.

He looked after its vanishing form. He saw ravens all the time. They were a plague on the newborn lambs. But it did seem as if this one were trying to tell him something. Hesitating just a moment longer, he followed it.

After another hundred yards, yet another hawthorn emerged from the murk. He hurried up to it. It had at some point— around fifty years ago, he estimated—split into twin stems. A combination of weakness and wind had brought down the nearest. The broken stump formed a natural jagged bowl full of rainwater. A few yellowed leaves floated on the mossy surface. He looked down and his reflection shimmered back, ghostly and insubstantial.

He studied the fallen trunk, dry and hard. He could see the grain clearly, and as he half closed his eyes and squinted, he could already see the trapped form of the beast within it.

He took out his mattock again. This time, as it touched the wood, he felt peace. *Trust your instincts.* This was the one.

It cut away easily, going willingly to its fate. When the piece was safely in his pocket, he laid his hand on the trunk and offered a silent message of thanks before turning for home.

Three days he had to spend on carving his talisman. Why, he had no idea. But the trapping ritual had to be held on the night of the full moon. That was the night after next.

What should he do? The instructions were meant to be followed exactly, but that would mean waiting another month until the next full moon. He couldn't do that.

Surely one day's difference wasn't that important? He could carve the head in two days easily. Should he do that, and undertake the ritual at the full moon? Or do it in three days' time, a day late? He stared at the still formless wolf's head.

He would spend two days on the carving, he decided. He couldn't see what difference an extra day made, but the moon may be important. He was sure it'd be all right.

Before he began carving, he needed to spend at least an hour in meditation. Purifying his soul. He settled himself against the icy stones as the chill sun hovered over Brownley Hill. He was well used to this, at least. The shepherd's life had taught him well.

He sat and watched the sun deepen into red as it sank lower. Thomas would never manage this. He still had a long way to go, to learn to be at peace with the world around him. As soon as he was away from that school, he'd realize then.

The chill prickled at his face as he breathed in the frosty scent of the fells. He could hear sheep near and far blarting as they settled for the night. A blackbird cackled in the valley as it claimed its roosting spot.

The sun touched the distant fell side, and he felt something else. It touched him, seared through him, surged through everything around him.

He held his hands instinctively toward the sun and felt its heat spark through his fingertips, his arms, down his spine and into the ground. He'd never felt this before.

Alive, in a way he'd never known.

The fells, the sheep, the blackbird. They were a part of him. Linked in an eternal web of life.

The sun became a sliver of red and vanished, leaving a red tinge in a rapidly darkening sky. He laid his hands down. The vision faded, but as he stood he felt it seething within him.

It was time. He was ready.

He went inside, settled by his fire and began to hew the rough outline. He stared at it, visualizing the form within which he would bring out.

He could see it perfectly. He'd never seen a wolf before, but from somewhere within him, its soul spoke to him.

Something shifted around him. The air became harsher, sharper. He looked around the room, saw Shep slumbering, the peat smoldering in the hearth. He was sure he could smell burning pine.

The stone walls flickered out of focus, moved outward, became smoother, rounder. Then he was looking out across the fells.

Not the same. He knew that at once. Far, far back in time, farther than he could imagine. Under the chill moon he saw the wolf pack, jostling each other as they raced across the heather. The leader stopped suddenly, stared toward him, ears pricked in a question.

Shep whimpered and the vision was broken. Bert was on his stool again, surrounded by stone walls, dizzy and disorientated. The flames had died down, as if an hour had passed. But he could still sense that gaze. Intelligent, inquisitive, smoldering with that untamable rawness that was the fells. He'd never imagined this. He knew it would define his creation.

He shut his eyes for a moment. He looked at the wood again, at the knife in his hand.

It had to be marked with his blood. To seal the bond between him—his soul—and the creation that would imprison the beast. The only way he could draw the beast inside it.

He held the blade against the back of his arm. Pressed slightly. His skin tingled. He steeled himself, then drew it sharply across. Blood welled and trickled down his arm.

He held the gash over the wood and watched the blood drip down. It splashed onto the wood and stained outward into the pale grain. More drops followed.

He stared. He could feel the world shifting again.

The droplets grew bigger. Pooled into the white linen, soaked outward across the bed. He couldn't breathe, couldn't think, couldn't do anything except clutch at Janet's hand, stare at her pale, ravaged face, too weak now to even cry out. He was dimly aware of the activity, of the women's urgent voices.

His fault.

She'd wanted to wait until they were married, but he'd persuaded her in the end.

She'd been three months pregnant when they were wed. Half a year ago. A lifetime ago.

If only, if only.

Janet jerked and a strange expression crossed her face. He heard whimpering and turned to see the woman cleaning mucus from the baby's face. Its face was swollen and blue. It was hurried away.

"Mr. Allenston. He needs to be baptized at once. What name shall I say?"

Janet's eyes drifted shut. It seemed so long ago, when they'd talked about names. Guy, after her father. George, he'd insisted.

"Mr. Allenston?"

"Guy," he heard himself say.

The priest's words came from far away. Minutes. Hours. He didn't know. The world turned black.

Bert realized his arm had stopped bleeding. The red had stained deep into the wood and dripped onto his trousers.

He scrubbed his arm with a cloth, focusing on the raw pain as the gash opened up again. He had to focus, although he could hardly look at the wood now, filled with the most terrible moments of his life.

He forced the memories back forty years and gripped his knife. He had work to do.

25

Bert put his knife down, flexed his aching fingers a few times, then held up his handiwork. The savage visage of a wolf glared back at him.

He narrowed his eyes and looked at it without blinking. He sensed the twitch of the nostrils, the ripple of muscles as the lips slowly pulled upward, the stirring of fur in the breeze. He saw his vision of two days ago, crossing centuries of time to touch him on the shoulder.

He opened his eyes fully again and put the carving down. No life was really trapped within the wood.

Not yet.

As was his habit, he stained the creature's eyes. A vivid blue, he decided. He'd never heard of a wolf with blue eyes, but for some reason it felt right. *Trust your instincts.* Then he wrapped it securely in a bundle of wool. It shouldn't be touched or even looked upon until the ritual was in progress. Wool at least, he thought with an ironic smile, was something he was well equipped to provide.

Next thing, he had to prepare the drink. This was supposed to free his spirit and enable him to both see the beast and do battle with it. Rowan berries; they of course were just outside. It seemed right to use those from Janet's tree, and he picked a basketful. They were slightly underripe, but hopefully that wouldn't matter.

The other things—mugwort, wormwood, broom—were trickier. He tried to think where he'd seen them growing in the valleys in the summer. Most plants had died down for the winter, but he managed to find a few wilted stems. At least they weren't covered by snow anymore.

It hadn't occurred to him before, but there was nothing in the instructions about keeping a stock of the ingredients. Perhaps at one time—like he now kept yarrow—it was simply routine for whoever guarded the secret to keep stocks of useful plants.

He boiled the ingredients in spring water until they formed a gelatinous red liquid, interspersed with flecks of gray. It smelled awful. He stirred it a few times, his stomach already twisting at the thought of having to drink it, then set it aside to cool. Shep planted his paws on the bench and sniffed the pan.

"Get away, Shep!" Bert grabbed hold of him and pushed him down. The last thing he wanted was him upsetting it. Or drinking it.

The dog dropped down and went to lie by the stove, head on his paws in a sulk. Bert went to the door and looked out. The sun was around two hours from setting. He'd have to leave soon.

A nervous lump formed in his throat and he breathed in slowly and carefully, forcing his nerves away. The light-headedness and the pounding in his chest he attributed to the day's fasting.

He'd decided on the location awhile ago. A natural spring down in the wood by the town. The Well of Saint Bride, it had been called in his youth. He was probably the only one who remembered that name now. Stones had been arranged to enclose the waters in a small pool before it trickled on. The beast couldn't cross water, apparently, like all beings from its world, so the spring would form an ideal prison once he had it trapped.

He remembered being taken there at Candlemas, or St. Bride's feast day, by his big sister Elizabeth and her friends when he was a bairn. St. Bride was the guiding influence for young women on that twin ordeal of their lives—marriage and motherhood. He'd watched the girls dropping early-blooming flowers into the water as they intoned the name of their desired sweetheart. All the girls used to come here, trying to see the face of the one they would marry.

Now, the path to the well was barely discernible. The stones were covered with moss; leaves and twigs filled the stone basin. No one had visited it for years.

He could hear the steady trickle of water rising up through the rocks, and he knelt and scooped out as much of the debris as he could.

The slimy mass seemed to spoil the harmony of the site, so he gathered it up again and carried it farther into the wood, burying it under some of this year's leaves.

When he returned the water was running freely, unimpeded by the detritus of time. It had washed away the remaining leaves, and he could see the bottom of the pool clearly. The trickling sound relaxed him. The shrine was restored. The ritual would work.

He knelt and looked into the sparkling waters. Saw movement. He bent closer.

He recognized her at once—her hair, her smile.

Janet was watching Guy by the sheepfold, playing with some wooden animals he'd carved. She looked so young, so alive. The pride in her face, as Guy stood on his squat little legs and toddled off. Above them, a raven circled.

Was this what could have been? Should have been?

Had she ever come to the well to find her sweetheart? Watched this same scene?

And it had all gone wrong. Bert couldn't stop a tear welling in his eye. He blinked hard. The vision was gone.

He started to stand, then saw a flash of red. As he bent closer again he saw Ellen, tired and thin, fussing over a perambulator. A fuzz of red hair beneath the blanket.

He felt a flash of pride that the Allenston trait had survived, although it looked like she hadn't carried the bairn well. There was a shadow about her, something black, miasmal, as if something had tainted her. He knew at once what it was.

And then he saw why.

He saw himself, talking to her, confiding in her. Telling her the secret.

The raven again, circling back and forth, back and forth.

It was nothing for a woman, he knew that. Especially in her condition. The consequences . . . He could never let her be hurt. He couldn't bear it.

He understood what he had seen. Knew what he had to do.

As Ellen leaned toward him, her eyes gentle and urging, as the words formed on his lips, he touched his hand to the water. The image shattered.

Bert shut his eyes for a second. She was safe now. Whatever happened, he'd succeeded there.

He stood up. The air was rapidly cooling now, less than half an hour until sunset. A blackbird was cackling deep in the under-growth. The water seemed louder now, as if to compensate for the deepening gloom.

He worked quickly, laying out the prescribed pattern on the ground. A five-pointed star with a candle at each point. He marked it out using ground chalk and salt, then enclosed it within a circle that touched each point. Three yards across, it had to be. He paced it out to check.

At each of the five points, next to the candle, he placed a single piece of rowan, hazel, hawthorn, heather, and oak. Then a raven's feather by each. Each one he'd had to acquire without causing harm, else their protective power would be destroyed. The four woods were easy enough, but he'd had to walk over a mile to find a broken stem of heather—high on the fell, battered by the last gale. He recalled where a pair of ravens had nested last spring, and found several feathers still under the tree.

Then he placed the carved wolf's head in the center of the pentagram, checking that it was equidistant from each point. He unwrapped it from its woolen shroud, careful not to touch it.

The blue eyes bored into his, and he realized the woods had fallen silent. The blackbird was quiet; not even a leaf stirred.

Gripped with a sudden panic, he blindly stepped backward, aware of nothing but the terrible pull of those eyes. It was as if it were alive already. He could feel the world shifting, sense the wolf of his vision padding out of time toward him.

He stumbled out of the circle and tripped. The gaze of the wolf's head was broken.

When he regained his balance he could hear the water running through the trees again. A slight breeze fluttered through the branches above him.

He looked around the clearing. The candles made the surroundings seem darker. There was nothing but a looming, empty gloom beyond their power. Was it out there, watching him?

Was that a flicker of movement he could sense, well out of reach of the circle of light? He had to hurry.

He pulled the bottle from his pocket and began to drink. It tasted vile, despite the honey he'd stirred into it. It was all he could do not to spit it out. He tried to gulp it down as quickly as possible, then gasped for breath. He swallowed a few times, trying to get rid of the aftertaste, then stepped back into the circle. His throat and stomach were burning and he was getting dizzier. Had he forgotten anything? He didn't think so.

He planted his feet in the northern point of the star, the rowan point, breathed a quick prayer, then drew his body up tall.

He lifted his chin and intoned the sacred words, the words of the old language.

"*Dewch yma. Dewch yma. Dewch yma.*"

It was the summons. The command that would draw the beast to the battle.

He waited, straining to see or hear any sign that it was working. Nothing.

He stood motionless, concentrating. Somewhere in the distance he heard a dog bark.

How long had he been waiting? He had no idea. He felt slightly sick and his left leg was trembling. Was that because of the drink? He didn't know.

He tried again. He said the unfamiliar words carefully, pronouncing each syllable as clearly as he could. Again, nothing.

His heart began to thump. Had he remembered the words wrong? Fifty years was a long time. He ran through every part of the ritual in his mind, just as he'd been told while sitting at his grandfather's feet so long ago. He was right; he was sure he was.

But what about his grandfather, or his father before him? Maybe they had remembered something wrong. Was all the carefully preserved knowledge worthless? Desperately, he tried a third time.

It was nothing definite. More a sense that something was there. A sense of blackness, a void lurking on the edges of his awareness. A faint rustling from the trees. The roosting blackbird took flight.

A thrill prickled over his skin. He felt a flicker of fear in the pit of his stomach, and then a calm readiness.

It was here.

He closed his eyes for a second. When he opened them again it was onto a new world. A greenish light bathed the trees, the glow of the candles penetrated deep into the gloom. The edges of the circle and the pentagram glowed a bright white, and a pulsating multicolored glow shimmered out from the pieces of wood and feathers. The carved head was radiating a pale blue light. He looked down and saw a stream of silvery sparkles drifting from his fingertips.

Beyond the circle, just on the edge of the ring of light, he could see an indentation. The circle was bowing inward. As he focused on that point, the indentation moved, beginning to circle around him.

"*Dewch ifi,*" he said, soothing, alluring. He traced a line in the air from the head to the shadow. The sparkles from his fingers coalesced to form a shimmering thread connecting the two.

"*Dewch ifi.*"

He carried on speaking the mellifluous words, and he thought he felt the beast sigh with pleasure. The thread condensed and he felt it draw inward, unresisting. It wanted it to be over. It wanted to go home. The ritual was working.

Just as it entered the ring of light, the movement stopped. The light was repelling it, he realized. It couldn't come any closer.

Carefully, he drew a new thread between head and beast. Using only his mind, he began to pull it inward, gently, carefully, so as not to alert it to his true intention.

Sweat began to bead on his brow and run down his face. He began to shake. It wasn't going to work. The ring of light was too strong. He couldn't draw it through.

He gasped for breath, holding tightly to the threads. There was only one thing he could think to do. He would have to break the ring to allow it to enter.

He left his spot, making sure he didn't disturb the threads, and went to the edge of the chalk circle. He'd been told he mustn't do this, but he could see no other option. And the beast was quiet, tamed. It wanted this to happen as much as he did. It would do him no harm.

Reaching out with his boot, he scuffed the chalk and obliterated a small piece of the ring.

Instant he realized his terrible mistake.

The ring of glowing white began to unravel, whipping around as if in a gale. The candles guttered and a gust of wind blew the circle of chalk dust into nothing. The pentagram remained intact, but Bert was now outside of it. He lurched back in panic, then stumbled and fell. He crashed to the ground next to the carved head, pain jarring through his wrists and hip. Then he saw with horror that his fall had snapped the fragile threads.

He grabbed the head, thinking to try and reconnect them, and the glowing iridescence blinked out.

The beast was free. And it was angry.

The illusion shattered, the beast saw the head for what it really was. It prowled closer and closer toward him.

Its invisible glare transfixing him. He couldn't move. All he could do was lie there, waiting for it to take its vengeance. He couldn't even feel afraid.

It circled again. He could feel its presence moving behind him. He shut his eyes and waited. He could feel the icy cold raking over him and his fingers began to numb. He'd failed. His responsibility, his duty, and he'd failed. He saw Janet's face in his mind. Failed.

He silently recited the prayer he'd said every day since he could remember, over and over, clinging to the familiar, soothing words. A faint candle glimmered in the darkness, wavering under the onslaught of the void. He concentrated on the light. On Janet's face. The bairn she'd never seen.

Thomas. Ellen. Everything he was fighting for.

The blackness was tearing at him with invisible claws. He clung on. He thought he could hear the cry of a raven, a flurry of frantic wings.

After an age, the storm eased.

He was aware of the leaf litter, cold against his face, and inhaled the pungent, earthy smell. He opened his eyes.

The candles were burned to meager stumps. The raven's feathers were arranged in a circle in front of his eyes. It sent a shudder of horror through him.

He pushed himself up and looked around. The head he'd so carefully carved was shattered into a thousand splinters. The beast was gone.

But he could still feel its taint, deep in his soul. It had seen him. And it would be back.

26

The winter was beautiful really, Bran thought. True to prediction, snow had fallen during the night and rapidly turned to ice, although it was nothing compared to what the Cailleach could really do if she wanted. He strode up the rocky slope, using his staff for balance on the icy ground. This was the highest peak in the area, and it also marked the midpoint of his journey to the lair of the cysgod-cerddwr.

He couldn't banish it. Not yet. He wasn't ready. But he could trap it in its cave until he was.

The slope leveled out and the wind, now unhindered, whipped gleefully around him and cut into his lungs. He pulled his cloak over his mouth as he paused. The peak had been used as a viewpoint for generations. Legend had it that it was here the Fomorii had first seen the arrival of his forebears. The irony was not lost on him.

He could clearly see that cursed road in the distance. Formed of laid stone, the road glowed a stark gray in the low winter sun, announcing its ugly presence and the presence of its creators. It slashed across the moor, arrow straight like a sword scar on a warrior's body. A symbol of division, in more ways than one.

And also, it was a symbol of the way forward. For people, for tribes, for countries. The thought surprised him. With a grudging admiration he saw the true reason for its creation. As Don had said, if one day he was forced to meet some of their priests, he would have to see them as equals.

As he studied the glimmering road, ignoring the vicious wind out of long habit, he made out a figure. He strained his eyes and decided it must be a journeyman or a trader. Moving too slowly, head down, bowed under the weight of his packs. Too normal, not at all like *them*. And they would never be out alone, anyway.

His toes were growing numb, despite the thick wool stuffing his boots, and he turned back to the trail. That the Pridani themselves were starting to use the road was a sign of defeat in itself. Convenient. Easier. Much better than the grassy trails they were used to—gentle and noninvasive but soon churned to mud by feet and hooves.

The symbol of division was becoming a symbol of compromise and adaptation. He knew then it was here to stay. That one way or another it would carry them into the future.

He glanced at the sun. It was only just past noon, but although the Long Night was nearly a moon past, the days were still short. He had to reach the cave before sunset.

A raven flapped into the air from behind a cluster of rocks as he passed, squawking indignantly at his intrusion. A second one followed. What were they feeding on? A sheep, maybe. But no sheep came this way.

He picked his way across the rocks until he saw it. A brown hairy leg, the skin torn in places, and then a section of antler partly encased in snow.

He knelt beside the carcass of the King Stag and laid his hand on the once noble head. The empty eye sockets met his gaze with an air of futility. *All things must have an end.*

He stared at it for a long moment.

When he stood up, it was with a growing sense of coming loss. Could he prevent war, provide peace? For his people's sake, he had to. He hurried on.

Downhill now, on the southern side where the sun had turned the ice to squelching grass. He covered a thousand paces in a short time. It was nothing compared to his years as a Wanderer, when he'd traveled from one coastline to the other. From flat, marshy land in the east which exuded chill gray fog, to the jagged black mountains scattered with heather and gorse in the west.

A lark flew up from just under his feet as he hopped over a bare outcrop. He slipped and twisted his ankle. He paused, flexing the pain away as he watched the bird singing wildly as it weaved through the air. It seemed to be a peculiarity of the species. He'd often observed them singing while in full flight from a hawk, and he had meditated on the oddity. He'd come to the conclusion that the hawk would abandon the chase much quicker when his prey had the strength to both fly and sing.

The lark decided he was not a worthwhile threat and fluttered quietly down to a rock where it began to preen. Careful not to disturb it again, he jogged on.

The grass gave way to thick heather. The woody stems deposited a layer of slushy snow over his legs as he passed. Despite his tight leather gaiters and boots, the damp soon began to seep through the seams. The woolen stuffing absorbed most of it, but he'd still expect to have blisters by the time he got home.

Another three thousand paces and he paused to drink a few handfuls of water from a spring. It numbed his fingers and burned its way into his belly. He wiped his hands dry and carried on. At the top of the next rise, he'd see it.

The cave was a slash in the hillside, gouged into the rock by an eternity of the Cailleach's winter torrents. He had seen similar caves with tunnels stretching two thousand or more paces into the hillside. He had no idea what awaited him here.

He pulled his raven cloak tight around his body, making sure nothing of himself was visible, then dropped the hood over his face. Entirely disguised by his totem, he moved silently and carefully down the slope.

He could feel it now. A sense of niggling disquiet, barely palpable to the senses but enough to warn away any casual intruder. He forced himself to ignore it, to concentrate on his footsteps. On the edge of his vision he thought he could see a gray mist exuding from the entrance.

Less than fifty paces to go. His fingers were growing white and numb. He painfully flexed his free hand a few times. He couldn't relax his grip on his staff.

A metallic tang on his tongue. He dabbed a frozen finger to his lips; it came back smeared with red. His nose was bleeding.

A twig snapped under his foot. Time froze. His stealth, his disguise, was shattered. No longer a fellow predator, the cysgod-cerddwr now knew exactly what was lurking outside its lair.

Although, he had the creeping feeling, it had known that already.

He forced himself to breathe carefully, deeply. The sun was still above the horizon. It couldn't harm him. Not truly. He flung his hood back, let the feathers flow down his back. Let his soul emblazon itself in front of the cave. Let the cysgod-cerddwr gaze upon its adversary.

He felt the challenge, and the acceptance.

He waited as the sun dropped lower. He no longer noticed the vicious cold, nor the needles seeping into his soul. Years of training quelled his automatic fear, the nagging sensation of silent eyes watching him, the illusion of stealthy feet padding toward him.

When the sun turned from orange to red, he crouched and opened his leather pouch. Pulled out a drinking horn with his free hand. He didn't dare let go of his staff.

Numbness crippled his fingers as he tugged at the wax plug, and he struggled not to drop it. He glanced into the empty depths. He could see nothing, yet. He laid his staff down. Felt the tug of loss at once.

It was a talisman, he reminded himself. An embodiment of the strength he himself had forged. He gripped the horn between the palms of his lifeless hands and tugged the plug free with his teeth. The sickly, metallic smell of blood rose up.

A black cockerel, killed at dawn. The herald of day had met its death as night had fled, and so the two opposites became twined. The blood would form an impenetrable barrier to all souls of darkness.

The blood had congealed since that morning, but he managed to lay an unbroken trail of stringy gobbets across the entire cave entrance. The first part of the ritual was complete.

The cold weakened slightly. Some feeling came back into his fingers as he reached for the bag again. He wasn't fooled. But he used his advantage to arrange three wax lamps across the mouth, each protected from the wind by a shield of birch bark. He took out the smoldering ember of bracket fungus he'd carried in a piece of horn and lit them. The light flickered tentatively inside the cave mouth.

It was too easy. He looked into the darkness again.

Darkness.

The lights had died.

The faintest flecks of hoarfrost lingered on the wicks. The flames had been frozen.

He seized the remaining ember of fungus. White bloom was spreading over the outer surface. He blew on it desperately and a spark of orange flared in the center. He stopped to draw breath and the frost spread farther. He blew again.

His chest was burning, his lungs almost empty. The ice was waiting.

A ray of the dying sun touched his cheek. A mote of warmth reached his mind.

His breath, his spirit, was feeding the flame. Spirit. Fire. They were the same.

As his lungs ran empty, he tipped the glowing ember into his palm and squeezed his hand shut.

The searing pain almost made him cry out. He had to grip his fist with his other hand to keep it closed. The smell of scorched flesh filled the air. He fought the pain spreading through his wrist and up his arm. Tried to focus on his breathing.

One breath. Two. The pain wavered.

Three. Four. It subsided to a throbbing ache.

He could concentrate now. Concentrate on the fire within him. Indelible and unquenchable, already trickling through his wounded hand to feed the dying ember. He breathed out and relaxed, letting it flow. His palm grew hot again, but this time with the soothing heat of a healer's touch. He opened his hand.

The ember glowed healthy and bright on the weeping, charred blisters of his palm. A fleeting pain as he tipped it back into its container and dropped to his knees in front of the lamps.

The flames melted the frost into minuscule droplets as he relit them. As he placed them down, white bloom crept up the bowls. The flames wavered.

His soul, he silently reminded them. *Unquenchable.*

They remained firm, melting the frost as it approached. He held them with his mind as he positioned them. Their light trickled into the cave.

He took out a paste of honey and ground rowan bark and dabbed it along the boundaries of the light. The pools shrank back, revived, shrank. *Unquenchable.* He held on to that truth. The barrier was complete.

He stood in front of the cave. As the sun touched the horizon, he stretched out his arms and channeled its power through his body and into the barrier. He began to intone the words to create an impassable boundary.

An invisible pressure tested the barrier. His voice didn't waver. The rhythmic pulse of his words writhed around the cave mouth, formed an impenetrable web that the cysgod-cerddwr could not cross. For now.

Snow, wind, and frost would eventually wear down his defenses, but it would hold until the full moon. And then he would have to be ready.

27

Bert shifted and clasped his hands behind his back, doing his best to appear unconcerned.

He glanced sideways at Ellen. She was looking more and more agitated. Looking from one side to the other, back toward the door, smoothing her dress to remove imaginary creases.

Stop it, lass! he cried in his mind. It was just drawing attention to her not-so-obvious but also very-obvious belly. A murmur rippled through the congregation, voicing the thoughts running through everyone's mind.

Was he actually coming?

Bert's smooth-shaven chin began to itch—he never bothered with shaving in winter—and the irritation niggled at him. After a moment he had to scratch it. He could feel rough patches of stubble. The beast had been out there again, last night. He'd heard nothing, but he'd *felt* it. Shep had been growling all night. And when he'd gone out this morning, another two sheep were gone. By the time he'd got back in after sorting out the carnage, he barely had half an hour to prepare himself.

Ellen looked toward him and he forced himself to smile casually. Her lip was trembling as she stared at him, but at last she managed to smile back. Both turned back to their long inspection of the altar.

He'd better be coming. Bert clenched his fists. *Hora fugit.* The words on the sundial outside came to him.

Somebody in the congregation coughed, the sound loud in the silence. It was quickly stifled.

The back of his leg was itching, but with so many eyes fixed on him he didn't dare scratch it. It had been years since he'd last worn this suit. Loose in places, too tight in others, with an underlying whiff of mothballs. He was more of an old man than when he'd last unpacked it, he thought with a familiar feeling of passing time. The belt buckle had broken as he'd done it up, and he'd resorted to twine to hold the trousers up. He glanced down discreetly to be sure his jacket disguised it.

Another shuffle and he recognized little Heidi's voice. "Mam! How much longer . . . ?"

A muffled slap on the legs and a gasp. He concentrated on picturing Maud's stern face behind him.

A creak from the ancient hinges and a gust of icy wind blasted into the church. Ellen's face split into a smile of utter relief. Bert thought she was going to rush down into her soon-to-be husband's arms.

Felton swaggered down the aisle, conscious of all eyes on him. His best man, a blond, shiny-faced boy Bert didn't recognize, didn't appear any less contrite.

Felton smiled at Ellen, possessive and dominant. Not loving in the slightest. Bert was now wishing he hadn't bothered to come, but Ellen was gazing into his eyes like a lovelorn puppy.

At least he looked quite respectable. It was always worth making the effort—a wedding suit could last a man most of his life.

Felton nodded to him and smiled hesitantly. Bert didn't smile back. Felton dropped his gaze. The vicar cleared his throat and they all turned to face him.

The ceremony was soon over, then the congregation gladly filed out of the cold, uncomfortable church toward the Hare and Hounds.

As Bert opened the door, the wall of noise struck him forcibly. Maud followed him in, the wrist of a pouting child gripped in each hand, her mouth a thin line. Heidi had a twig in her hair and a smear of mud on her best frock. They were hauled toward the kitchen.

The room was stiflingly hot after the church. He stood in the doorway and looked around. He could hear shouting men, the hysterical giggle of a young woman, a girl's squeal. It sounded almost like Heidi. Had she escaped her mother's clutches already? He looked back longingly at the peaceful heights above the town, then sighed and shut the door.

The dim light and close atmosphere closed around him. He could feel his throat tightening. He tugged at his collar but there was no way to loosen it. A thousand itches began under his shirt and his trousers were digging in around his waist. Oh, to be in his normal clothes again. But he'd probably only wear this suit once more, and then he wouldn't be in a condition for it to bother him.

The laughing entrance of the newlyweds was greeted with cheers. Felton's arm was possessively around Ellen's waist. Any minute he'd throw her over his shoulder like he'd won a pig at a fair. Bert edged away.

He glanced up at the clock. Nearly five hours until sunset. Five hours until his daily nightmare began.

He pushed through the throng to the trestle table, nodding to a few people, and got a piece of bread and butter. He chewed mechanically as the throng eddied about him.

"She's pregnant, you know."

A woman's voice in the crowd. The bread turned to ashes in his mouth.

He searched the crowd and spotted Hilda Pinkerley, her hand conspiratorially on another woman's arm. Mary Berry, the farrier's wife. Crumbs fell to his plate under his tightening fingers.

Mary's eyes lit up with gleeful excitement. "Really? Now that's a surprise."

Anger rose in him. He felt like pushing his way over, knocking the teacups from their hands.

"So soon after the last, too." Hilda shook her head with exaggerated concern.

Bert let out a breath he didn't know he was holding. They weren't talking about her.

"The bairn can't be more than six months old. She'll never manage, you mark my words. It's this fancy milk powder that's done it. You don't fall when you're feeding, my mother always said."

"But she couldn't feed him herself, could she? Ill, she was. Got the fever after the birth. Look, there she is now."

He followed the direction of the two gossips' eyes. Alison, Scruffy Joe's wife, was making her way toward the women.

"Alison! Wonderful news you're expecting again!"

He saw Joseph was helping himself to bread and butter, his hair uncharacteristically tamed. He began to thread his way toward him. Bert braced himself.

Whatever Joseph had to say, Bert could tell he wasn't going to like it.

28

"Four ewes, three yearling lambs. A half dozen more gone without trace." Joseph shook his head. "I've never known anything like it."

Bert shut his eyes for a second. "I've lost twice that number, this week alone."

Every night, it was there. He'd put up lanterns, set traps, stayed out all night with Shep. But it always came. It was a small mercy that it only came in the night.

"What are we going to do about it?"

Bert couldn't think of an answer.

Ellen waltzed up to them and he forced himself to smile. He couldn't let his worries mar her day.

"Uncle, you must have some of Maud's cake; it's delicious! You, too, Joseph. I've brought extra big pieces." She handed them both china plates.

As Bert took it she placed her hand on his arm. "Don't worry so, things will work out." She looked at him pleadingly. "Try and forget about this wolf for a while, or you'll make yourself ill. I want you to be happy today."

He should have known she'd see straight through his smile. She was too sharp by half.

"I am happy, lass."

He held her at arm's length and this time his smile was genuine. She looked bonny, she really did. Forget-me-nots, her dress reminded him of, and it barely showed the swelling of her belly. "I'm so happy for you."

"I knew you saw the good side in Jack. He's a good man; he really is."

Was that a statement or a wish? She looked earnest for a second before the overjoyed, nervous, and slightly bewildered look of all brides returned. He squeezed her hand.

Joseph coughed. Bert looked at him and saw his eyes were fixed on her belly. Their eyes met and Joe's eyebrow twitched before he busied himself with picking cake crumbs from his plate.

Bert wished for a moment he could take her away, protect her from the prying eyes and gossiping whispers. It wasn't fair. Women shouldn't be subjected to things like this.

But there was nothing he could do now. She was married, no longer an Allenston. And Felton had done the honorable thing. Eventually.

He tried not to think about the coming birth. As always, his Janet's ravaged face swam into his mind before he forced it back with trembling worry.

Heidi charged past, squealing, another girl just behind, and both men had to step back. A couple of boys were chasing them. One caught Heidi's pigtail and tugged the ribbon free. She squealed even louder. *There's jam on your skirt, and butter on your sleeve,* he thought. Bed without supper for you tonight.

Ellen patted the little rosette of flowers in her hair. Yellow gorse, which looked striking against her red hair. He remembered the old saying, *Kissing is only permitted when the gorse is in flower.* Of course, gorse flowered year-round.

"Ellen, pet! You look amazing! That's a beautiful dress. Did you make it yourself?"

Alison came up and kissed her cheek. They plunged into an animated conversation about those things only women were interested in or understood. He caught Joe's eye and they shared a wry smile.

Felton approached and hesitated. Bert stepped back to make room for him. A silent look passed between them.

"All right, lad?"

Felton pulled the lapels of his new suit together, pushed his hands into his pockets, immediately removed them. Bert took a bite of cake. Ellen was right, it was very good.

"Mr. Allenston, um . . ." Felton looked awkward, then blushed.

Bert glanced at Ellen. The women were poring over the cuff of her dress. He heard "turned lace" and "loop stitch."

"Mr. Allenston, I just wanted to say . . ." Felton met his eye for a second then focused on the floor. "You were right, you know. I'll look after her. I promise."

"Make sure you do." A statement, an encouragement, a threat, he wasn't sure.

Felton looked at him, obviously wondering the same. He fidgeted for a moment, then backed away into the crowd.

Ellen had been watching the exchange, Bert realized. Did she know what had been said? He hoped not. He awkwardly concentrated on his cake. Alison went off toward the teapot.

A volley of hoots and cheers across the room. Felton was gulping down a brimming tankard, surrounded by a group of young men. Ellen looked over as well. She was no longer smiling.

"He's a rum 'un," Joseph said quietly. "Pity she let him have his way with her."

Bert felt a rush of protective anger. Angry with Joe, angry with Ellen, angry with Felton. Angry with the rapidly disintegrating world.

"She's only a lass, Joseph! He's the one to blame. She could have done better, I know, but she'd be worse off in the poorhouse."

Joseph raised his hands in apology and Bert regretted his outburst. Ellen joined the group of lads and Felton slipped his arm around her waist. He pulled her to him as he laughed with the others. Ellen gazed up at him, almost blushing at the brazen contact, but he didn't look at her. She said something but he pulled away and took another proffered tankard.

Bert pushed his way over and took hold of the tankard. The ale sloshed over the side.

"Your wife's talking to you. You ought to be listening."

Felton looked bemused. They stared at each other for a moment, and then Felton let go of the tankard and threw his hands up. "All right, come and dance, darling." With a sullen backward glance he pulled his wife away.

Several people had fallen silent. Bert handed the tankard to the another man and pushed toward the door.

The square was deserted. Everyone was in the inn. He leaned against the wall, glad of the space and fresh air. A flurry of sparrows descended to squabble over some spilt corn on the muddy cobblestones. He watched them for a minute. He ought to go back soon. He shuddered at the memory of last night's carnage, despairingly wondered what he was to witness tonight.

He could stay a while longer, although Lord knew he didn't feel like it. As the sparrows fluttered away, he sighed and turned back to the door.

Maud was sitting primly upright just inside, hands clasped in her lap in a perfect decorous posture. He supposed he ought to be polite.

He sat down next to her, then deliberately slumped back and stretched his legs out. Maud looked at him with disapproval.

"Her father wouldn't have approved, of course. Edward scrimped and saved to put money aside for her betrothal. His one wish was to see his daughter decently married. He'd turn in his grave if he knew." She sighed. "Those years without a mother, I fear. A girl needs a strict guiding hand, something a man cannot give. I told her the Allenstons didn't marry the likes of the Felton family, but she wouldn't listen."

Bert looked at the throng. Maud was quite right, but the lass still deserved support.

"I wonder when she will bear a child?"

He looked at her warily. Was she alluding to Ellen's unborn? He wasn't sure. She'd married late—she'd been well over thirty—but she'd had children of her own. She must have noticed the signs.

She gave him a thin-lipped smile, tinged with bitterness. "May the Lord keep her womb empty. That Felton will do little enough to support them, mark my words. She'll have to scrimp and slog to feed and clothe them herself."

Bert stared at her. He couldn't believe she'd say such a thing. But then, widowed with two small children, it was very difficult for her.

"Come what may, things will come right in the end." He hoped he was right.

They sat in silence for a moment. He looked across at little Katie, sitting quietly on a bench, hands folded, legs swinging, a pink ribbon in each pigtail.

"Katie looks like a little doll," he said. He felt sorry for her as he traced her envious gaze to the other romping children.

"Her name is Catherine." Maud smiled, taking his comment as a compliment, as he'd suspected she would. She stood up.

"Tea, Bertram?"

He agreed, and she glided through the crowd to the table. Samuel Gatesby dropped into her seat.

"Heard the news? His lordship's bringing in some hunter, a big game hunter, to try and kill this wolf. He met him in a club in London. He's hunted wolves, tigers, even elephants. They're saying he'll make short work of it." He chewed his thumbnail. "I hope they're right. It's left my sheep alone the last week, but it could be back at any moment."

Bert felt a familiar sense of hopelessness. It wouldn't help. Of course it wouldn't. No one could do anything, except him. And he'd failed bitterly.

"You don't think it'll work?" Samuel read his expression.

"Does he know these fells, this hunter? Does he understand the lay of the land, the way the spoor lies on the grass, the movements of the winds? Does he know every trail, every spring and drinking spot, every place the deer lie up? No, he doesn't. No one does but us. And we've searched and found nothing. He'll not stand a chance."

Samuel nodded slowly. "But something has to be done."

Bert knew that. But he'd tried the best he could, and he had no idea what to do next.

29

"Hiding away as usual, when you should have been here!"

Judging by Coll's face, he'd been seething for hours. Bran strode past him through the gates. Fearn was standing in a quiet huddle with a few of the other men. Not enough to indicate anything serious had happened.

A flicker of movement and he saw the silhouette of Mintana keeping watch on the wall.

"What's happened?" he asked Fearn.

He'd known as soon as the village came into view that something had occurred; torches lent an orange glow to the night air and a hum of voices betrayed the men's wakefulness, despite it being well past midnight.

"A party of the invaders came, a few hours before sunset," Fearn answered. "They wished to trade for food."

"You spoke with them?"

"They do not speak a civilized language!" Coll appeared in front of him. "Their savage tongue no one can understand but themselves! As regimented and unnatural as the men themselves."

Bran struggled to remain patient. "Then how . . . ?"

"They had an interpreter. One of the southern men, who has taken to their ways. He speaks their language perfectly and made their case for them."

"A treacherous leech he was, too. I sent them away. I told them we have no food or anything else to spare for feeding dogs." Coll spat the last word.

Bran raised an eyebrow toward Fearn, who shook his head slightly. "We have little enough to spare, that's true," the hunter said. "But it may be better to cooperate for now, else they may return with more men and simply take what they want."

"No! We treat them like the dogs they are. The Cailleach is reminding them whose land they are in, and they are not to forget it!"

"Sometimes, Coll, a little thought is needed preceding important matters." Bran's voice was icy, and clear enough to be heard by all those loitering in the shadows.

The other man froze, and Bran could feel the anger and resentment rolling off him. He held his gaze in the dim light and dared him to speak again.

"The invaders have gone, anyway. They wanted to reach the fort at Coria before dusk," Fearn interjected. "But their interpreter remains here. He understands our ways, of course, and he said he would speak to the Pennaeth when you returned."

"I told him he would have a long wait. The Pennaeth of the Pridani has far more important matters to attend than listening to the half-baked pleas of traitors and foreigners." Coll was looking up at the half moon as he spoke, a trace of bitterness in his voice, and Bran allowed himself an inward smile. Despite his failings, the smith's loyalty toward his people was unquestionable.

"So where is this man now?"

Fearn gestured toward the Meeting Hut. "He is waiting, anxiously." He chuckled mirthlessly.

Bran pushed aside the hide covering and ducked inside, the other two men following.

The man jumped to his feet and turned to face him. His back was to the hearth so Bran couldn't see his features clearly. He crossed to the other side of the hearth, forcing the man to turn. Now illuminated by the firelight, Bran could study him closely.

He was dressed warmly in the normal wool and fur garments. He hadn't adopted the ridiculously impractical and inadequate garb that the invaders were reported to wear, Bran noted with both satisfaction and disappointment. He'd been hoping to see their clothing close up. At first glance, he looked no different to any of them.

But still, there was something different. A sense of regimented order in his demeanor and general appearance. His hair and beard were carefully trimmed, his cloak held by an unnecessary number of toggle fastenings. There was a definite sense of order about him, the obvious influence of the invaders.

"I am Belinus," he said when no one else spoke, his eyes flickering over the raven's feathers, which danced orange in the firelight. He licked his lips. "I am working on behalf of the Romani, who want to trade with the Pridani."

"So they can build more forts and take the land that is ours?"

Bran was aware of Coll nodding, his massive arms folded deliberately across his chest.

"A peaceful compromise that is of benefit to all." Belinus glanced at Coll and licked his lips again. "They bring foods, cloth, spices, and wine from their faraway land. They build fine roomy houses."

He faltered. Obviously he wasn't convinced by his own pitch. Their houses, as Bran well knew, were hopelessly inferior to their own, suited as they were to their balmy southern climate.

"They bring trade," Belinus tried hopefully, "and build roads."

Bran snorted. "All the better to spread their plague. We have no need for these cursed roads."

Belinus's eyes flickered from him to the other two men, waiting in the background. "So what is your answer? Are you prepared to trade?"

"It's nearly a moon since the Long Night. We barely have food enough for ourselves."

Coll smiled grimly and took a step closer. "You have your answer; now get out."

The interpreter hesitated, still watching Bran. "And in the future? In the spring, and the summer?"

Bran looked at him for a long moment. The room stilled as everyone waited for his answer.

Yes, and they would become like cowed dogs, ever obedient to their masters' whims. *No*, and war, devastation, and death would be followed by the exact same outcome.

Could they ever fight these invaders? Could they ever live with them? The firelight flickered and danced.

"Yes," he eventually said. "We may be willing to trade."

"What?!" Coll pushed around to face him and Belinus recoiled. "You cannot sell us to these leeches! We will not submit to their demands. I will not let it happen!"

His face was mere inches from his own, and Bran's vision was filled with flaming red hair, framed by the glowing firelight behind.

"You have no idea how to lead the people, Bran. You have no idea about anything."

Fearn made to step between them but Bran waved him back. "I'm telling you, this is our only option. The only way we will survive."

He held Coll's gaze. He could feel his breath on his cheek.

"Tomorrow, a meeting. For all the village. They will decide for themselves whether my decision is right."

Coll nodded slowly and stepped back. "That they will indeed. They'll want to hear a better story, too. And that they will as well!"

He turned and strode away, flinging the drapes aside and disappearing into the night. The room seemed immediately empty.

"Belinus, you require shelter for the remainder of the night?"

The man shook his head. "I will leave now. There is moon enough to travel, and as soon as I reach the road it will be very easy going. Wonderful things, these roads are." He flashed him a sly look.

"Thank you for your hospitality, Pennaeth of the Pridani," he continued formally. "I will pass on your answer. I'm glad you're wise enough to make the right decision. You won't regret it."

That was debatable, Bran thought tiredly as they walked together to the gate. "Safe journey," he said as they went their separate ways.

30

The Christmas meal was presented with a flourish. The lamb tasted champion—tender and succulent from a lifetime on the hills, seasoned with rosemary and wild garlic and smothered with rich gravy. The only sound now was the scraping of knives and forks on plates.

"You've surpassed yourself this year, Helena." Bert mopped at the last of his gravy with a piece of potato.

His daughter-in-law beamed and Guy squeezed her arm. "All thanks to you, Dad. It's you that rears the lambs so well. And Thomas as well, now." He glanced at his son and the boy grinned self-consciously.

Bert leaned back. The children had gathered sprigs of holly to decorate the room, and the berries glowed a warm red in the firelight. The candles flickered and danced. He felt his worries floating away on the smoky haze. The attacks had lessened slightly over the last week. Only four sheep gone in five nights.

Three-year-old Sophie was rocking on her stool, impatient for the rest to finish. Bert could feel the table wobbling. He began to twist his fingers into shapes to amuse her. A grin spread across her face.

"And how about young Ellen? I wonder how she's found her first two weeks of married life." Helena's tone suggested she knew exactly the answer.

"I have serious doubts about that young man," said Guy as he carved the second helpings.

"Yes, but in her situation—"

"What situation, Mam?" Claire and Rebecca both looked up. The sixteen-year-old twins already had a woman's infallible nose for gossip.

Helena didn't answer. She was a rare jewel in that respect.

"Mam? What?"

A blast of wind crashed into the window. Sophie screamed. "The monster! It's coming!"

"Sophie! Sit still! Of course there's no monster!"

"What's this about a monster?" Bert asked her with an indulgent smile.

"It's Micky Pinkerley," Thomas explained. "He's been telling everyone stories about the demon in Hell's Mouth that they've let escape. He says that's what's been killing the sheep."

A candle guttered and died. In the eddy of smoke, Bert thought he saw a pair of eyes looking at him. Everyone knew the stories about what was trapped in Hell's Mouth. Everyone had always avoided the place, reminded by regular reports of hovering lights, spectral screams and legions of marching soldiers, until someone from away discovered it was full of lead ore.

Did the stories link to the beast? His grandfather hadn't known. It suddenly seemed very likely, although the revelation would be of little use to him now.

"Micky's saying it got out when they were blasting. The rock came down and there it was. Massive, black, fangs like razors. It could have eaten him."

"That's enough, Thomas." Guy glared at him. "You're scaring Sophie even more. I'll have to have words with that boy."

"I was just saying . . . !"

"Quiet, all of you. Not today." Helena stood up to begin clearing the dishes. Claire and Rebecca leaped up to help. Bert pushed his thoughts aside and found himself checking Helena's body for signs of yet another pregnancy but was relieved to see none. He always had several worry-filled nights around her confinements. It had been three years now, and she was nearing forty. Perhaps her childbearing days were coming to an end.

He remembered the relief when Thomas arrived after four girls. And when the next three had also been girls, Thomas became the pride of the family. When Guy had had to forfeit his future, Bert had found himself wondering if he was to be the last of the line, but his grandson had changed all that.

Eight was a fair brood, and all surviving infancy as well. But then, the Allenstons had always been prolific. He himself had been the youngest of nine—six older brothers and two sisters—and his father had been one of thirteen. People used to ask, very seriously, what the old man liked to do with his spare time. Bert realized his father also had six elder brothers. He'd never noticed that before, but it made him the seventh son of a seventh son. It had quite a ring to it.

He thought about Janet then. She'd be so proud to see this brood, the legacy of her life.

"Dad? Pudding?"

Bert realized everyone was looking at him. "Er, yes, please."

Guy was looking at him, his brow furrowed. "It'll be all sorted out, when this lion hunter chap gets here. Stop worrying so much."

Bert nodded silently. With an effort he forced himself to concentrate on the plum pudding. Guy pushed himself up and began to hobble toward the hearth. Claire jumped to her feet.

"I'll do it, Dad. You sit down."

Guy squeezed her shoulder and turned back to the table. His leg was always bad in cold weather.

"Thomas will be finishing school soon," Bert said. "He'll be coming to work with me, then?"

It was posed as a question, although the boy's future had been decided long ago.

"He'll do you proud, Dad."

Guy's confident smile was tinged with sadness, Bert noticed. Their eyes met and Guy rubbed his leg.

"All my family have done me proud," Bert said quietly.

"What do you say to that, Thomas?" Helena prompted.

The boy shuffled on his chair and looked at his plate. "I was wondering . . ." He scraped up a trace of pudding. "Maybe I could work on the railways or something."

The room grew still. Even little Sophie was quiet. Guy glanced at Bert.

"Of course you can't. And where do you think the money's going to come from for a position like that?"

"You need to get these fancy ideas out of your head," Helena admonished. "Be grateful with what you've got. A good, secure future, like many boys would dream of."

Thomas was scarlet. Bert had to smother a smile. He'd heard it so many times before. That was school, he supposed. They learned to read and write, and they thought they could do anything.

"Tommy looks like those red apples!" little Sophie giggled.

The tension was broken. Everyone laughed.

"Have the last helping of pudding, Dad." Guy threw a final glare at his son.

As he chewed he bit something hard. He pulled the silver sixpence from his mouth.

"Make a wish, Grandpa! What are you going to wish for?" All the children were looking at him eagerly.

He thought of the past, and the future. He looked around at ten members of his family. Eight of them were to live their lives in this new century, where the world he knew would be swept away. What would their lives hold in store for them? He looked at Thomas, wishing he could see what was to be.

"I wish . . . ," he said. "I wish . . ."

31

The wind was vicious today. As Bert surveyed the broken wall, it whipped around him and drove deep under his clothing. He could see consecutive swathes of wind hurtling across the fell side toward him, bowing grass, heather, and trees as they passed.

Thomas came up beside him, hands deep in his pockets and his chin tucked into his jacket, a futile attempt to defend himself against the snarling teeth of the fells.

"Don't you ever hate this weather? I can't wait for spring."

"No use complaining about it, lad. You can't change it, so just get on with it. Moaning gets you nowhere."

"Don't you ever wish things could be different?"

"Things are the way they are. That's just the way it is."

Bert twisted to keep his back to the wind. It didn't help. Maybe he needed a new, thick jersey. He'd still not got his boots sorted either.

But like he'd just said, no use complaining. He looked across the fells. Where was it? It was out there somewhere, taunting him with its absence.

"Grandpa? What are we going to do?"

Thomas jerked his head toward the stone blocks strewn on the frosty ground. Bert had forgotten for a moment what they were doing there.

"It needs repairing, of course. It blew down last month." He stamped his feet and blew into his fingers.

Thomas nodded. "I remember that gale. It took the slates off Widow Jenkins's house. Left a great big hole in the roof, it did." He jiggled about. "Why haven't you mended it before? Weren't you worried the sheep would get out?"

Bert shook his head. "This is their boundary, the edge of their territory. They're hefted to this part of the fell."

"'Hefted'? What does that mean?"

"It means wherever you take them, they'll always find their way home."

The wind blasted a spattering of grit against Bert's face. He bent and heaved up one of the biggest rocks. It was painfully cold on his hands. "To work then, lad. Soonest started, soonest finished."

They began to position the stones back into the wall. Bert soon got into a rhythm. He kept an eye on Thomas's efforts. It was looking good.

When he judged it was noon he rolled his shoulders back. Shep looked up from the chunk of wood he was chewing.

"Dinner, lad."

Thomas dropped his stone with a smile of relief. How long had he been waiting for him to say that?

"Down where those two walls come together." Bert pointed and led the way. He clambered over and Thomas vaulted to join him.

"It's so warm here!" Thomas exclaimed.

Bert grinned. One of those strange quirks, the warmth of the sun was trapped and the wind deflected. He sat down gratefully. Shep settled against his legs. He warmed his fingers against the dog's skin.

Thomas wiped his hands on his trousers and unwrapped the food. Bert took the coarsely sliced bread, slathered with butter and thick honey. The rich, pungent flavor took him back to the balmy, sunny days when the air resonated with humming among the heather. He shut his eyes and saw the deep purple swathes stretching across the fell side. Nesting curlews wheeled and cried incessantly. He breathed in the warm scent of the flowers and felt the breeze caress his skin.

Thomas nudged him a moment later. "Grandpa! Wake up!"

He regretfully opened his eyes. He must have dozed off for a minute. He licked the last trace of sweetness from his lips, sighed, and pushed himself to his feet. The wind whipped around his face with glee.

"Come on, then. Back to work."

Their rhythm broken, it was always much harder to get going again. Without pausing to think, Bert lifted a good-size stone. Icy grit stung the warmed chaps on his fingers.

As they toiled into the afternoon, he watched Thomas surreptitiously. Cold, sore, tired. This was what sorted the men from the boys.

The boy was obviously struggling. His hands were soft and delicate, more suited to knitting than proper man's work. That was what came from years wasted in a schoolroom. Bert could see they were growing red and sore, and Thomas's face was getting increasingly strained.

The boy picked up a stone and braced it against his stomach. It slipped from his grasp and clipped his foot. Bert winced. Thomas leaned against the wall, pressing his injured foot against his other leg. His lips trembled.

"All right, lad?"

"Can't we go back soon?"

"We've got a job to finish." Bert picked up another stone.

"But it's so hard! The stones are freezing; they're cutting my hands to pieces. My arms ache, my feet are completely numb, and now that one's nearly broken." Thomas was almost in tears. "It's horrible up here. Can't we do it another day?"

"Snap out of it, lad. Just stop feeling sorry for yourself. To get anywhere in this life, it needs damned hard work. Grit and sweat. Now stop whining and get on with it."

Bert turned his back on him and carefully slotted a stone into place, taking much longer than necessary. He could hear the boy sniffling behind him. Just as he thought he'd have to challenge him again, he heard him shuffle away and pick up the stone he'd dropped.

Bert looked at the descending sun for a moment to hide his face. He had to be harsh. It was a tough life, and only the tough would make it. He wasn't going to do much more, anyway.

"Look, there's some fur on that stone, like a dog's! Is it Shep's?" He pulled a tuft of it away and held it against the dog.

Shep snarled and stepped forward. Thomas backed away, his mouth open in shock.

"Shep! Stop it!" Bert poked him with his boot.

The dog's mouth snapped shut and he slunk back against the wall. When Bert looked at the stone, he understood.

He could feel an inky blackness stretching up from the fur toward his fingers. A chill spread through him as he stared.

It had been here.

Why had it been so careless? But he knew it hadn't. It was taunting him. *I'm here, and there's nothing you can do about it.*

"Grandpa? Are you all right? What's the matter? Grandpa!"

He looked around. Thomas was looking worried, almost panic-stricken. The tuft of fur drifted to the ground.

"Someone's dog's been this way. That's all. Let's get back home."

As they crested the hill, a rumble came from somewhere out east. It reached a slow crescendo before fading away.

"Was that from Hell's Mouth?"

Bert winced. When was this damned hunter coming? If nothing else, it wouldn't come near if he was around.

"They use something to blow up the rocks; all the better to get the lead out." Bert spat and strode faster.

"Dynamite, Grandpa. It's called dynamite. A gentleman came to inspect the school last week. He's called Mr. Richmond," Thomas said, panting as he struggled to keep up. "He told us all about the new ways of mining, and the factories and quarries. He said soon there'll be roads across all the moors, and railways, too. The countryside will be opened up for industry instead of wasted on sheep. We won't have to walk across the fells anymore, and everything will get so much easier for us."

Bert looked away. These beautiful fells, torn apart by roads and rattling wagons, by shouting and blasting, he couldn't bear it.

"It'll be amazing, won't it, Grandpa?"

Suddenly, he felt very old. "I suppose it'll happen."

"Mr. Richmond told us about a 'scholarship.'" Thomas pronounced the word carefully. "We can take exams and maybe go to the grammar school in Hexham, where they wear a uniform and everything. And it's all paid for. Even working-class boys like us can work in the new industries.

"I could work as a mine foreman. A train driver. I want to work in a big iron mine. Mr. Richmond said industry's the future. We won't have to live on the fells anymore, we won't have to just keep sheep. He said new doors are opening all the time."

Bert felt like smacking him. Why could the boy not just accept what he'd got?

But this wouldn't be for the likes of him. If all the boys left, who was going to tend the sheep?

"I'm practicing my reading. I read in the newspaper they've found a lot of lead in Hell's Mouth, and they're going to build a new road across to get it out. It's going to bring a lot of revenue"— he looked at Bert knowledgeably—"to Allendale." He caught hold of his sleeve and tugged him to a halt. "I'm going to do it, Grandpa! I am. I'll make you so proud of me."

"Come on, lad. Sun'll be set soon."

They walked toward the top of the hill. Shep ran ahead, sniffing through the heather. A grouse flew up and bumbled through the air. Thomas laughed at its insulted chortling *chu-chuck chu-chuck*. The bird crash-landed in a boggy depression, stumbled onto its beak, regained its balance, and scarpered into the heather.

"When I was a lad, my brother Henry met a boggle just there. He was going to see his lass, Mary Yates from down in the vale. He thought he saw her standing the far side of that bowl, but she took no notice when he called, so he walked down there. Of course, it's proper wet down there, and it'd been raining, too, so in no time he was up to his knees in filth, and in his best clothes as well.

"Of course it hadn't been Mary at all, it was just the boggle pretending to look like her. Poor Henry heard it laughing as he was floundering in the mud. Mother was so angry when he got home, peat and muck all over his Sunday suit."

Bert wiped tears from his eyes as he remembered. He'd almost forgotten what it was like to laugh.

"It used to take on all sorts of shapes to cause mischief—animals, bundles of wood—but that was the first time it took the form of a girl. So be careful, lad. If you see something that doesn't seem right, it probably isn't. And you ask Scruffy Joe about the Wooley boggle!"

"Mr. Richmond said things like boggle are just uneducated superstition. We need to move on from things like that."

Bert stopped laughing. He felt like he'd been kicked in the stomach. How dare he speak to him like that?

"Come on and get back home," he said sharply. He whistled to Shep and strode off.

He reached the top of the slope, still seething, and stopped. The valley opened out below them, stretching toward Allendale and beyond. The tenuous warmth of the sun was rapidly fading and Bert could feel the cool evening air prickling at his skin. He leaned on the wall and gazed outward.

On the highest fells, a smooth white sheen blanketed the ground. Everywhere was tinged pink by the sun, now a dull red orb above Brownley Hill. Sheep bleated in the valley as they settled for the night, and much farther away the rooks cawed as they jostled in the trees.

He breathed in deeply, the chill catching the back of his throat, and smelled the scent of pine. The burn was trickling far below them and he could hear Shep padding about, then sitting down for a scratch.

He glanced at Thomas who was leaning on the wall as well. He caught his eye, silently. A shared moment of perfection, there was no need for words. All hostility was forgotten as they listened to the song of silence, the music of the fells.

The sun touched the horizon and began to sink. The sky erupted into a soft pink, and all sounds died away. The whole world seemed to be watching.

Thomas was absorbed. The look of peace, of wonder, on his face said it all, and the same feeling spread through Bert's own heart. Everything would be the way it was meant to be. With Thomas, with the future, with everything. All this talk of leaving, the boy's heart was here. The fells flowed through his blood and his soul sang the song of the hills. How could he ever leave it all behind?

The last distant sliver of red vanished. The sky gave way to a deep blue and the glowing white began to turn gray.

Bert pushed himself up from the wall. "And thus ends another day."

32

Bran watched as Beth picked her way through the growing crowd, her movement labored and ungainly. Coll's arm was proudly around her waist.

Someone offered her a seat and she lowered herself down. She had barely half a moon to go. He was surprised she'd managed the climb to his lodge a few days back. He looked at her face but she refused to catch his eye.

She was wearing an iron brooch on her cloak. One of Coll's new creations. The twisting, weaving design, flanked with wrought leaves, was simply stunning. It was prominent on her breast, but she was trying to hide it with her hair. Coll would have intended it to be more than a symbol of his skill. It was a declaration of battle.

Amid the shuffling, coughing, and hushed excited voices, the crowd swelled. A few latecomers—shepherds and cowherds letting their wards loose to graze—and then the entire village was present.

Waiting on the higher ground in front of the gathering space, Bran carefully gauged the demeanor of the group. Coll and Beth were a little way off to his left, Beth fidgeting in an endeavor to get comfortable. Fearn was close to hand. Mintana was sitting cross-legged by his feet, looking up with solemn importance and gnawing on an apple. It wasn't often that the youngsters were included in Pridani meetings.

Bran shifted position and leaned on his staff with both hands. A subtle gesture that drew the attention of all present. They fell quiet.

"You all know why we are here," he said. "It is time to accept that our land is changing."

His words were answered by a ripple of breeze through the thatch of the surrounding buildings. All eyes were fixed on him.

"It is clear that the newcomers are here to stay. We cannot hope to defeat them. We only have to look at what's happened to the Iceni and the Brigantes to know that."

The children were staring wide-eyed at him. They understood it was a turning point in their lives but were too young to understand how. Among the adults, he could see anger, disbelief, denial.

He continued, carefully choosing his words. "One cycle, one turn of the wheel, is coming to a close. A new time is dawning. If we, the Pridani, are to continue into this new era, we will have to adapt. Accept. Change. If we try to fight, we will be crushed. This is our only chance. Our only hope for the future."

He could see Coll was growing angrier. He shifted from one foot to the other, crossed his arms. Then he pushed forward.

"Just because you haven't the skill to do anything but cower like a beaten dog! Why you were made Pennaeth, I'll never understand. You're just selling us out to them. You'll have us all slaves in our own land. You can't get rid of the beast that's attacking us, and you won't even try with the invaders."

Several people in the crowd looked at each other.

"No, Coll. They will win, eventually. And at what cost to us?"

The anger within the gathered people was palpable. Bran stepped forward slightly.

"The invaders will not be here forever. And neither will we." He projected his voice so the entire gathering could hear. "The world changes, and the people have to change with it. Lives end, so new lives can begin. You all well know that our history tells that story."

A murmur with an undercurrent of uncertainty. They had wrested the land from the Fomorii, a fact that lingered uneasily in their minds. It could all too easily happen again.

Bran looked pointedly up at the Clenched Fist. Everyone followed his gaze.

Coll strode forward, stood slightly in front of him and turned to face the crowd. The sun was behind him and made his hair gleam like fire. A good position. Coll could see and judge the faces of the crowd, but with the sun in their faces they couldn't read any weakness in his own. Bran too subtly adjusted his position.

"We need new weapons, better and stronger, equal to what these foreigners have!" Coll shouted. He'd never learned to project his voice well. He just sounded angry.

"I've been testing new techniques this last moon. In my new furnace, I've made iron blades better and stronger than ever before. Stronger than the invaders' blades. They will defeat them!"

He paused deliberately. A masterful move. The crowd's focus changed. Bran saw the interest, hope, and respect reflected in the massed faces.

"We need a Pennaeth who has strength!"

The crowd drew in closer. Bran could see people glancing at each other. His mouth grew dry and he moistened his lips. Fearn quietly drifted to his side, Mintana next to him.

"Coll, you're wrong," he countered. "It's not just weapons we need. The invaders surpass us in every way. We're just like . . ." Bran looked across the hostile faces, his fingers tight around his staff. "We are like wasps attacking a bullock. They sting, and they die, but the animal is none the worse for it. We none of us have the power to defeat them."

Coll's face grew triumphant. "But what about my baby? Beth's baby?"

All eyes turned to her swollen belly. She looked around uneasily.

"The Horned God himself gave her his essence! My blood will be the future of the Pridani. My baby will lead us into the future. What does that tell us about who should be Pennaeth?"

A murmur of agreement. More people moved to Coll's side.

"He is going to be the greatest Druid in the land!"

"No he won't, Coll."

A sinew in Coll's arm twitched and his hand strayed to the knife in his belt. The crowd glanced at each other again. A few looked worried. Bran waited just a second longer.

"But *she* will."

Coll looked puzzled for a moment, his fingers still on his knife hilt. And then the tension was broken. His face broke into a stunned grin and an excited conversation started in the crowd. Beth grew red as she was suddenly the center of attention.

Everyone knew the stories, and everyone understood what his words meant. A daughter of the Horned God, born into their own people. She would be the embodiment of their land, in a way nobody had been before. Her descendants would be a part of the land forever. Their future was secured, a chain forged by the Gods themselves that could never be broken, no matter what was to happen in their brief lives.

So it mattered not which of them was Pennaeth now. Both their times were at an end, so that *her* time could begin.

Bran allowed himself an inward smile, and he felt Fearn's silent touch of congratulation. Those three words were all he'd needed for them to understand his message.

33

The last bright star winked out and the sky turned abruptly red, as if swathed in blood.

Bert slowly eased his grip off the gun he'd borrowed from Joseph, his knuckles throbbing as the tension released. His eyes felt like they were full of sand, his back was smarting with pain racing up his spine, and his feet were frozen and numb.

He squeezed his eyes shut, the ache lessening slightly, and sought relief in the darkness behind his eyelids. He was tired, so tired. He felt himself drifting into sleep as he stood. He stood for another couple of seconds, then forced his eyes open.

He went around the fold and extinguished each of the lanterns, which were supposed to keep it at bay. The sheep inside looked up at him mutely. No stretching, no eagerness to greet the day, no waiting at the gate for their first bite of grass. The beast was sapping the strength of his flock in every way.

He opened the gate carefully so the jagged tin he'd nailed to the top didn't cut his hand. It was a futile deterrent. His flock slowly edged toward him. Molly looked up at him, twitched her ears and shook her head. *I know you're doing your best,* she seemed to say as they straggled out. He counted them out, hoping and dreading. The last one left and his shoulders sagged.

Not again. How could it have happened?

He checked around the walls. Nothing. Perhaps he'd counted wrong. But he knew he hadn't. Two missing. He looked around the walls, topped with wood, wire, tin, anything he could get that was hard and sharp. Nothing should be able to get in.

But it had. And he'd heard nothing.

It was all hopeless. He'd tied bundles of rowan twigs at each corner of the fold; iron horseshoes as well. On impulse he'd wedged iron nails between all the capping stones. He remembered when he was a bairn, the older women said the blacksmith was the only hope against the Wee Folk, and they put nails under their cribs to guard them.

He'd taken from the beams upon which they still hung the plaited straw angels his Janet had spent summer days making. He stroked the dusty straw with a calloused finger, wondering if the memory of those magical days would help.

It didn't.

He'd bound it to him, and nothing would stop it returning. He kicked at a stone with his boot, the impact jarring his leg even through his numb foot.

Shep was whining at the door, frantic and forlorn. He rushed out, sniffed Bert over, then relaxed under his caress. Bert hated to leave him inside, but what else could he do? The dog was so vulnerable himself.

His eye alighted on the feeble excuse for a wolf's head he'd attempted to carve. A rushed and botched replacement. He knew he'd already lost. There was not a flicker of life in it; even he could see that. The beast would never be fooled.

He picked it up and hurled it. It hit a bush and the sheep nearby bolted for safety. That made him feel even worse.

He went inside, poked at the cold ashes in the hearth. He'd been gone so long even the last ember had died away. He slumped to the floor. Shep crept under his arms, and he held him tightly and shut his eyes.

The banging on the door woke him. He looked around blearily, wondering why he was on the rug. His mouth felt full of mulch and his eyes stung. As he struggled to his feet the door opened and he was struck by a rush of icy air.

"Grandpa! Guess what?"

Thomas bounded into the room, slammed the door behind him, then stopped. "Grandpa, what's the matter? You look awful. Has the wolf been back?"

Bert nodded weakly. Thomas gave him a look of sympathy.

"That's what I've come to tell you. That hunter, the one his lordship's bringing up, he's here! He'll kill it for us now. He's got huge guns, far better than those of Cousin Joseph's, and he's coming here now! They went to Mr. Gatesby's in a motor car."

The boy hopped from side to side. "It's amazing! Big and silver and black. I'd love to have a ride in one! But anyway, Mr. Gatesby said you had the worst of the problem, and they should see you instead. So they're coming now; they'll be at the track soon." Thomas looked at him expectantly.

Bert rubbed his eyes and went to the door. The sun was high and the sheep were white grazing dots.

As they walked down the hill Shep, who was running on a short way ahead, suddenly froze, one front leg in the air, and stared toward the rowans. A low growl emitted from his drawn back lips.

"What's the matter with him?" Thomas looked the same way.

Bert felt a chill come over him. That's where he would find them. The ones that had gone. He'd take his lordship and that wretched hunter over there and show them just what the problem was.

"Look, he's here!"

The rattling, coughing motor car, belching smoke and fumes from its rear end didn't really need announcing. Thomas was staring as the motor car eased to a halt. A few children were racing up the lane to see.

Bert stopped and waited as the two gentlemen began to extricate themselves. Thomas stood at his side. His lordship approached, flicking his walking cane in front of him.

"Allenston. I hear you've had a spot of bother with a wild beast."

Spot of bother? Spot of bother? Bert's hand tightened on his crook. He saw himself driving it into his lordship's pampered, perfectly shaved face.

"Gatesby tells me you've had the worst of the problem; are there any dead animals for Mr. Bigley to inspect?"

Bert took in the leather jacket, the carefully polished boots, and the flamboyant hat that the big game hunter sported. Already he was having to hold the hat as the wind whipped around them. The pompous, city-bred prat would get absolutely nowhere.

"There were two last night, over by the rowans." He gestured, turned, and strode toward the trees, not waiting to see if the men followed.

"Have you hunted lions, sir?"

Bert gave Thomas a whack around the head, but Bigley turned to look down his nose at the boy. "I have, my boy, and savage ones, too. Man eaters: they killed two of my own men." He smiled disdainfully. "Their heads are on my wall. Your little problem should be easy."

Thomas's mouth fell open. *Grandpa, I don't want to be a shepherd. I'm going to hunt lions.* Bert walked faster. He could hear his lordship breathing hard as he struggled up the slope. Bigley, though, he seemed to be coping with the pace, he thought with a grudging respect.

He found them immediately. On the grass, as if specially laid out. Thomas cried out as he saw them. Bigley went up to them, careful not to get blood on his polished boots.

Of the first, there was a head and nothing else except the skin. Even the bones had gone, crunched up by immensely powerful jaws. The second was nothing but skin, the wool matted with red, and a thighbone, gleaming white. A strange smell of burned iron mingled with the stench of blood.

Bert steeled himself and looked at the eyes of the first, still retaining their expression of absolute terror, then turned away. Jack-in-the-Box, the ewe that had so amazed Thomas by jumping up to eat the ash leaves that day. He recognized the markings on her face.

"*Hmm,* yes, well, quite." His lordship looked shocked.

Bigley prodded the remains with an experienced air. "Yes, I've seen the likes of this many times. A wolf, definitely."

"A wolf would not have eaten the bones, sir."

Bert saw the flare of anger in Bigley's face. "My good man, I have hunted animals around the world. I know more about wolves than you ever will. Kindly leave me to make the judgments."

"Mr. Bigley is a good friend of mine, Allenston. He's doing us a great favor, coming to help us with this problem. So, what do you propose?"

"I and my outfitter will search for trails and lairs." Bigley waved his hand in the direction of the fells. "There's always scope for local help, of course, but I feel in this case there will be no need." His gaze traveled disdainfully over Bert and the massing crowd down by the motor car.

"There'll be plenty of places for it to hole up—cave, rocks, and the like—up on those hills. Then I'll lay bait in likely places, and when it comes . . ." He smiled grimly. "Its head will soon be adorning my wall."

"We've already searched for its trails and lairs," Bert said, but the gentlemen were already walking off, satisfied with their plan.

He went to fetch a shovel to bury the remains.

34

"I still think we need to fight them, Bran. They're like dogs. They'll never give up until they've taken everything we have. What's happened in the south says we have to fight. Better die in battle than die as starving rats."

Bran handed Coll a cup of mead. "They can't afford to waste many warriors up here. They're stretched to their limits already. Let them build their forts, let them build their roads. They'll crumble to dust eventually. Nothing lasts forever."

Coll nodded slowly as he looked into his mead. It was as if his unborn daughter had already doused his temperament. Would the babe have that strange red hair? The two men sat in silence for a while, lost in thought.

"How are you going to imprison the cysgod-cerddwr? I can forge a wolf's head if you need me to. As real as life itself."

Bran looked at him. Coll's face was sincere and open. He'd almost forgotten how much Druid training the smith had done. The wolf was the closest earthly likeness to the cysgod-cerddwr, but there would be no need to create the entirety of its form. The head was the seat of the soul, of life itself. That was why so many otherworldly beings could only be destroyed by decapitation. So many stories had now become legends, but all were based on truth.

"I'll carve it with stone. I don't doubt you can do it, but I have to create the image myself."

Coll nodded. "If you need anything, just ask. It's a hard battle to fight alone."

He'd misjudged the smith sorely, Bran realized. A humbling thought.

"There was something I was thinking of. A better tool for working the stone."

Coll sat up straight. "Tell me."

"Like a chiseled blade, but curved to reach the inner surfaces. Flat and blunt on one side, sharp on the other. I'm not sure how it would be done. But I must start the work tomorrow."

Coll was looking at the smoke hole with his eyes half closed. "I can see it. It would be difficult, but I can do it. The furnace is still hot; I'll have something for you by morning."

Then he was gone. Bran looked at the closing door drapes and shook his head. What had it taken to finally reconcile them? But it had happened when it most mattered, which was the important thing.

When Coll returned to his lodge the next day, he'd forged the tool even better than Bran had envisioned. He'd added a curved handle as well, for better control. Why hadn't he thought of that himself?

Coll was looking at him with barely suppressed pride, and they clasped hands.

"Thanks, Coll."

When Coll left the lodge, Bran began his preparations. By the time the sun was close to the western horizon, he was nearly ready. He placed his bear's skull on the post outside his lodge. Took one last look at the village below, and closed the drapes on the door, submerging himself in darkness.

Three days of isolation. Three days of fire and rush light. Three days to form the prison of the cysgod-cerddwr which that contain it safely in this world forever.

No one could disturb him. The task involved himself, his totem, the ancestors of the Pridani and the Gods he called upon. If these forces were disturbed, the reprisals could be severe. The skull, radiating the winter sun, was a warning. People would glance nervously at his lodge and make the sign against the evil eye. Mothers would hush their children, cowherds would still their animals' bells, all fearful of some malign attention.

Bran lit four bowls of beeswax, finely worked so they barely guttered, and positioned them around the lodge. The darkness retreated toward the eaves. He glanced around, but they weren't here. Not yet.

He threw the dried stems of wormwood and mugwort onto the fire. The parched woody stems flared up at once and the pungent aroma filled the confined space. The smoke tingled his throat and lungs as he took the pot of simmering water and prepared his drink. Infused with wood sage, beech fungus, hazel, and yet more wormwood, sweetened with plenty of honey, it would open his eyes to see the inherent image in the stone.

He turned to face the fire and began to sip his tea, making a point of relishing every drop. Already he could feel the familiar buzz as the honey entered his blood and the magical components of the plants wove themselves into his soul.

To create an image of anything, whether with stone, wood, paint, or metal, was to capture a part of its soul. But this task was far more intricate than that. He couldn't just create an image of the beast's soul. He would need to capture the entirety of it.

To do that, he had to create a likeness so good that the beast, separated from its body in another realm, would be fooled into believing it had found its home.

And when it was drawn longingly to it, he could bind it so it could never again escape.

Bran studied the block of stone he'd selected. Durable, eternal, but also easy to shape and carve. He half closed his eyes and visualized the form of a wolf emerging from it. He let his mind drift and watched the head turn, look at him, then tip back and howl. Somewhere far in the distance across the fell, another wolf answered. The jaws snapped shut and the eyes again met his in challenge.

He reached out his hand to touch the virgin stone and the wolf's form retreated. But it was in there, waiting.

This wasn't a task he could do alone. He began to speak, drawing down the powers of the spirit world, invoking the ancestors from their eternal slumber. Calling all those who would aid him in his task.

As he uttered the final invocation, the fire hissed. Flames surged upward as if a burning branch had split open. The shadows dancing around his lamps took on shapes, twisting and writhing, drawing closer to him. He concentrated on his heartbeat and the heartbeat of the earth.

"Who calls us? Who disturbs our peace to draw us back to this world of death?"

The words, cold as the midwinter wind, unforgiving as the moorland crags, brittle as a splinter of ice, came from everywhere and nowhere.

"I am Bran, Pennaeth of the Pridani," he silently answered.

The flames shivered.

"The cysgod-cerddwr must be removed from this land. It is not a being of this world. I require the assistance of those from beyond the veil. You must lend your help."

The shadows crept closer. A sharp chill stroked his neck, along the vein that took blood to the skull. He knew not to flinch.

The pressure grew sharp. A popping sensation. He could feel blood coursing down his neck, his chest, pooling into the earthen floor.

"The Pridani must be freed from the cysgod-cerddwr. It must be imprisoned, and your power will strengthen its bonds. Three days, and then you will return to your land of life."

His voice was calm. He couldn't allow the slightest suggestion of weakness. He concentrated on his breathing, on the pulse of life echoing around him.

A smell of earth, of decaying leaf mulch. The blood loss made his head spin. He had to fight not to slump to the floor. The shadows crept closer.

"Lend your strength to my knife. I must begin work at once."

The words took all the strength he had, but they were cold and clear. The pulsing blood was dwindling to a lethargic trickle. Sparks danced across his vision. He couldn't hold on much longer.

A sensation like a bubble bursting. The blood stopped flowing. The shadows writhed about him. Over the aroma of the burning herbs, the lodge was filled with the delicate perfume of beeswax.

Bran touched his hand to his throat. Clean. Uncut. He smiled.

He picked up the stone, arranged his tools about him, and began to work.

It took him a day to shape the rough outline. Only his innate senses, the tides of the sun and moon flowing in his blood, told him of the passing time.

He put down his tools and gazed at it through the smoky atmosphere. Blurred, indistinct. But he could see the nascent form of the cysgod-cerddwr emerging from the hazy stone, drawn outward by the spirits he had summoned.

But every action caused—needed—a counterreaction. For the carving to capture the soul of the cysgod-cerddwr, it would also need a part of his own soul.

He felt a shiver of disquiet. He laid his hands on the stone, watched the surface ripple under his fingers. Something in his mind urged him to tear them away. He could feel the invisible touch of the spirits, like the brush of a spider's web, reaching out of the stone to grasp them. He forced himself to submit.

He knew what was needed. His memories, his past. The moments that had made him who he was.

The time was clear in his mind. As he recalled it, he saw it forming in front of him, a shadowy scene drawn greedily into the stone.

He was ten years old. Old enough to have known better.

It was Samhain night, and he looked at the deserted, dying bonfires with the thrill of a boyish dare. Embers pulsed in the cold breeze. A charred branch suddenly blazed up. He could smell the rich, fat meat still lingering around the empty spits.

He glanced around for observing eyes and sought what he was looking for. Luisa, the Pennaeth, was a smith of phenomenal talent. She had forged three iron ravens for the Samhain rituals, and Bran had the strange, overpowering urge to gaze upon them. He'd slipped from the village walls at near midnight, after everyone else had safely returned inside.

He'd almost turned back, more than once. Cringed at every rustle, every snap of a twig. He knew what lurked the land on Samhain night.

He could see them now. They gleamed black, red, white, in the firelight. He caught his breath as he looked up at them. He could feel the strength in the talons gripping the poles, hear the breeze ripple through the feathers, outspread for balance.

Sense the predatory gaze upon him.

He stepped back, his mouth suddenly dry. Looked over his shoulder. The village walls seemed a long way away.

He looked up at the nearest raven again. It met his eyes impassively.

It had moved. Turned to face him. Its wings were drawn in, ready to swoop.

He stepped back, spun to see the others. The same. One bobbed its head slightly.

The realization rushed over him. The sickening understanding that everything that lurked in the depths of his every nightmare was real. As his every security was ripped away, the three metal birds screamed toward him.

35

The stick pounding on the wall post broke him sharply from his trance state. The image shattered.

"Bran? Bran, I must speak with you. There is a problem."

He recognized Coll's voice. The man was both foolhardy and very stupid.

He stared desperately back at the shimmering air. Only fragments like teardrops remained. Could he recover it? He knew how hard it would be.

He eased his hands from the stone. A sucking sensation as his past—and his future—were released. He took a moment to recover his presence. There was no further sound from outside. At least the smith was not so foolish as to try and enter.

He took a sheepskin and covered his work, his tools, and the discarded chippings, making sure there was nothing left in sight, then blew out the candles. The shadows retreated to the edges of the lodge, out of sight. He went to the entrance and pulled back the hides a fraction. The piercing sunlight of a new dawn made him shut his eyes, tears rising sharply.

"Come in, Coll." His voice was harsh and cracked after a day of silence. He withdrew back into the gloom.

Coll hesitated, then ducked through the drapes. The darkness retreated for an instant, then flooded back. Bran watched him as his eyes grew accustomed to the gloom. He looked at the wax lights, still smoking, at the sheepskin with its unknowable contents. His nostrils twitched at the powerful herbs in the air and his eyes flickered around the shadows of the room. He made the protective sign against the evil eye and his eyes came back to Bran with nervous dread.

"Bran, it's Beth. She's not well. She's bleeding. Too much, the women are saying, and it's still too early. We've tried raspberry-leaf tea but it does nothing." His eyes were pleading. "It's because it's such a burden, the babe of a God, isn't it? If she can't birth her . . ."

Bran's mind was still lingering in the trance world. He forced himself to concentrate. Coll had given her the remedy everyone was familiar with, but he was right. In her case the burden was too much.

"She must rest. Keep her lying down, so the weight of the babe doesn't push itself free."

"Yes, I made her do that. She wanted to make more swaddling clothes, but I said that can all wait."

"Give her an infusion of motherwort. And goats rue as well. Boil the leaves, add honey, leave it to cool, and then strain it."

He went to the chest, where he kept his stocks of herbs and found the two plants at once. He handed both pouches to Coll who tucked them into his cloak with the merest tremble in his hands.

"Don't worry. If she wasn't capable of carrying the babe, the Horned God would not have chosen her as his vessel. They both will be healthy and well, but panic will taint her womb. Faith, Coll. Faith."

Coll swallowed and nodded. "I just don't want anything to happen to her."

The fire spat and made him jump. He looked around nervously. "I'd better go. How goes . . . ?"

Bran nodded without speaking. Coll turned to leave.

"Is there any other news?" Bran asked.

"Don came back. We told him we will make no decision regarding war until the spring. He didn't like it, but he accepted your decision." Coll smiled with an easy confidence Bran hadn't seen before. Their eyes met for a second, then Coll turned toward the entrance, raised a hand in farewell, and was gone.

Bran turned back to his fire and relit the lamps. When he'd settled his mind back into its hypnotic state, he removed the sheepskin.

The memories coalescing around the stone were tangled and fractured.

Panic. Terror. A nightmare plunging toward him.

Cold eyes, gleaming red. A window into a world of macabre, writhing shapes. He screamed as he ran, plunging through the ashes, uncaring as the embers seared his skin.

Empty moorland. He'd gone the wrong way. He spun around as talons pierced his shoulder. Razor-sharp pain as blood flowed.

Empty moorland. The same. He sprinted every way, any way, always toward nothing.

He could taste blood. Smell blood. Hear a howling more terrible than the scream and clash of warring armies. He saw the chaos of blades and shields. The shadows swallowing the slain.

Torchlight. Grass. Ashes. He was scrabbling toward nowhere.

Luisa pulled him up, gripped his face between her hands and stared into his eyes. He couldn't remember what she'd said, what she'd done. But then he saw again the dying fires, and the three ravens perching silent on their poles.

They were the totem of the Morrigan. The Dark Goddess. The Lady of Crows. The Carrion Eater.

He now had a choice.

The visions had marked him. *She* had marked him. She had shown him what lay beyond the veil, in worlds where only Druids ventured. He had received his calling.

His choice. Heed it, or walk away.

He understood honor, duty, prestige. He understood the power the Druids wielded.

He understood the terror as his mind had been flayed open.

He was ten years old. He accepted his calling.

Every day, every ordeal, every terror he had to face, he was reminded; it was his choice. He could walk away, any moment he wanted.

He never ran away again.

And eventually, he knew he never would.

The memories wound themselves into the stone. Drawn inward by the spirits that hungered for them. He watched them go, smiled grimly. This was who he was. This was who would defeat the cysgod-cerddwr.

He slid his hands from the stone and picked up his tools. It was time to bring his creation to life.

Another day dawned and died before he prized his stiff, dusty fingers from the handle of his blade. He flexed them and a sharp ache shot through his hand and wrist. He blinked and looked at the wall, struggling to focus. He felt light-headed and dizzy, and pain throbbed in his temples.

But he'd done it.

The shadows swirled expectantly and the air hummed with tension.

"Your assistance was invaluable," he said formally. "I and the Pridani and the future Pridani thank you."

He blew out one lamp with a sharp breath. Some of the shadows died away. The vibration in the air eased a little.

"Return to your realm, to your eternal rest."

He blew out the second lamp.

"Your duty is fulfilled, there is no need to remain."

He blew out the third. The hum, already far away, spoke of something unfulfilled.

"Until we one day meet again, in the land of the afterlife."

His voice betrayed no emotion. A debt was owed. And he knew what the price would be. He blew out the fourth candle.

The last shadow vanished and the disquieting presence was finally gone. The hut was now lit only by the glowing embers in the hearth. He made up the fire high and when it was blazing brightly, he held up his creation.

The fierce eyes of a wolf stared back at him. Its ears were pricked, the hairs carefully defined. The lips curled back in a snarl, the fangs acutely prominent.

The eyes, though, were dark and empty. The stone was not alive.

Not yet.

36

One night of peace. One night without loss. That Bigley fellow must have done some good, trooping up the fell with three men to carry his guns, netting, and snares. He'd set up camp across by Chat's Fell, in a spot he'd decided was out of the wind. "Obviously that's the direction the creature's coming from," he'd said.

He'd have seen nothing, of course. But neither had Bert. The man had warned it off, if nothing else.

The hunter had rigged up some fancy cloth net, supposed to disguise him and his army from all unwary eyes. Bert looked up and saw the net, fluttering in the breeze, clearly visible in the growing dawn. He couldn't help but laugh. How he'd managed to shoot as much as a sparrow in his career, he didn't know. He laughed until he was bent double with weakness. One night without it. He'd never felt so good.

Thomas was coming up the track. The boy searched his face for news.

"It didn't come last night? I saw Mr. Bigley's camp up there. He could shoot it easily, I think. Has he?"

Bert shook his head. "No, lad. He hasn't caught a whiff of it." He started to laugh again.

They both looked up the hillside to where a figure was emerging. It stretched, looked toward the rising sun and began to walk down toward the road. His outfitters started to pack up his kit.

"Off to his lordship's parlor for port and kippers, no doubt." Bert shook his head. "But anyway, we've got hurdles to make."

By midafternoon they'd got a good stack done. Thomas had managed three. Not bad for a first attempt. Bert twisted the final willow lath around on his last hurdle.

"How's it going, lad?"

Thomas glanced around, and the lath he was struggling to bend snapped.

"I thought it was going well!"

"Never mind. You've done a good job." He pulled the stopper from the bottle of cold tea and took a swig. Much better warm, but no chance of that in this weather.

He offered it to Thomas, who shook his head. "Ginger beer; that's what I like."

Bert smiled indulgently. "Got to learn to like tea, lad. You won't get on in the world unless you do."

Thomas checked his hands. Bert almost winced at the blisters across the bases of his fingers. And the boy hadn't complained once. He didn't let him see his smile of pride.

"Those willows"—Bert gestured as Thomas picked at a blister—"will be ready for coppicing next year. We cut them every seven years—willow grows fast. Hazel and ash need much longer to regenerate."

The boy wasn't really listening. He was focusing carefully on his work. Bert swigged some more tea.

"Grandpa? What would happen to Cousin Ellen if she wasn't married?"

"What do you mean?" The words came out cold and harsh.

Thomas blushed and wouldn't meet his eyes. "They say she should be going to the poorhouse. Would have done if Jack hadn't married her."

"Who's saying that?"

"Mrs. Pinkerley. I heard her when I went to the butcher's for Ma."

That damned nosy shrew.

"Ellen is respectably married. Her baby will be born legiti-
mately. You'll do well to remember that."

Thomas concentrated on his hurdle for a moment. "But why?
Why do women have to be married when they have children?
Why can't they be like the ewes and rear them on their own?"

Bert could hardly stop himself laughing. "It just doesn't work
like that."

"But why not?"

"Women need a man to look after them."

"Why? Are they stupider than men?"

"Not as such. But they can't do the hard work that men do,
obviously."

"They couldn't run twenty miles across the fells. They'd be trip-
ping over their skirts the whole time. But you live on your own.
And Aunt Maud lives without a husband. I'm sure one day it will
be done."

"Maud's a widow; that's different. If she could find a husband
who'd take on another man's children, she'd remarry in a day." Bert
looked up at the sun. "We'll take these hurdles back now, then
fetch the ones on the fell. We'll be keeping the sheep close to home
for now."

They set off up the hillside. Bert could barely keep up with the
boy, he realized with dismay and pride.

He thumbed the familiar contours of the wolf on his stick, and
Thomas was still admiring the grouse's head on his own. He'd been
as delighted as he'd hoped with his gift. Now he was a shepherd
proper.

"Mam said you'll find it hard soon, living on your own. You'll
be much better off when I'm living with you."

Bert snorted. "There's still plenty of life in the old dog. At least
she's not saying I should move into town."

Thomas grinned. "She wouldn't dare. But with your bad hip
and everything . . ."

"All the more important you get away from that school and up here, eh? You'll make things a lot easier for the old man."

Thomas was silent, staring across the valley. A skylark floated up on a wave of song.

"When Grandma died"—Thomas searched his face—"why did you never remarry? Dad says you were very young. And then you'd have lots more grandsons than me."

It was Bert's turn to be silent. He remembered the joy, the hope, the worry, the despair.

His fault.

The thought of it happening again.

"Sorry, Grandpa. I didn't mean to upset you."

"I loved her. I could never replace her." He turned away.

"Come on, let's get home."

The sheep were waiting in a huddle at the fold gate. They got them penned in, the gates secured, the lanterns lit. There was nothing to do but wait. The ground was hardening and a mist of swirling condensation materialized from their breath. The familiar feeling of dread began to rise as Bert saw the first stars appearing in the deepening blue. Would it come tonight?

"I ought to go, Grandpa. Will you be all right on your own?"

He nodded. He couldn't risk the boy getting hurt. "That Bigley fellow's out there somewhere. Assuming he isn't sipping port in his lordship's drawing room. He should scare it away."

"You don't think he'll be any good?"

"Of course he won't. Guns and traps are useless." He stopped himself.

"But he's hunted lions! He'll get it, Grandpa. I'm sure he will."

"We'll see. Get off home now. I'll see you in the morning."

"I can't." Thomas didn't meet his eyes. "It's Monday, I need to go to school."

Bert's never-ending worry boiled over.

"What nonsense is this? Stop wasting your time with all this reading! You need to be up here, learning something useful." He stabbed his crook into the ground and felt it flex under the pressure.

"But this scholarship, I really want it. I can do well, really well! I'll make you proud!" Thomas stared at him desperately. "You said life needs damned hard work, and that's what I've got to do."

"Don't you swear at me, boy!" Bert was shaking with anger. "Look at everything you've got, everything you've been given. And you just want to throw it all away. Your future, your *responsibility*, is here on these fells! Not in some town. Not in some mine. It's time you learned to understand that."

"Grandpa, it's you that doesn't understand!"

"No, Thomas!"

They glared at each other. Shep began to whine. They both looked down, and the dog crept to Bert's feet.

"I'm going home." Thomas turned and strode off, beginning to run as he reached the track.

Bert knelt and rubbed Shep's neck, watching Thomas disappear into the twilight. He had the horrible feeling that something was disappearing with him, never to be seen again.

37

The sound was heart-wrenching. You'd never think a sheep could scream, but scream she did.

For a horrible moment, Bert thought it was Molly. He grabbed his crook and ran. Where was that damned Bigley?

Of course, wherever the beast wasn't. It would make sure of that.

They were already scattered, the gate hanging from one hinge, but he could see the white bundle against the wall, smattered with dark brown. Blood just looked dirty at night.

He rushed toward it, although he knew it was too late. He ignored Shep's frantic barking. The beast, visible only as a void, an empty space against the background, moved. Crouched down, ready to attack. He didn't care. He just wanted it to leave him alone.

It was tensing. He raised his crook. The shadow lunged.

Something hurtled past him. The momentum as Shep ploughed into the beast was enough to knock it off balance. The shadow slewed to one side but still an immense weight crashed into him. He spun and fell hard. Spots of light danced in front of his eyes. Something punched into his ribs and a searing pain spread through him as he tried to force air into his lungs.

He could hear barking, was aware of another sound, indescribable but terrible. He wasn't sure if he was really hearing it. More a primeval feeling, of *nightmare*.

Shep. Where was Shep? He had to get him away from here. He tried to call him but no sound would leave his lips. Now, he felt afraid.

He struggled to move, found he couldn't. His legs refused to obey him. His fingers reached out but just slid uselessly along the icy ground. He could feel a warm wetness running down his cheek. A hellish chill crept over him. He tried to look around but could see nothing but blackness. Were his eyes open? He couldn't tell.

A roaring filled his ears. Ravenous teeth tore at his soul.

Around him, above him, strange metallic birds glared down from wooden poles. Ravens. He stared in terror as they turned to face him.

One flicked its tail and stooped, then all three hurtled toward him. He tried to scream as something unnatural, primeval, savage—even more than the beast—devoured him.

The rush of a thousand wings. A screeching he recognized. Ravens, fighting over a barely dead carcass. He tried to cover his face, his eyes, squeezed them tightly shut, although it wouldn't do any good.

It did nothing to lessen the vision before him. He was surrounded by them. The world he knew faded before the onslaught.

He felt as if he were being lifted in the air. Feathers fanned his face.

He'd heard of angels carrying the saved to heaven. He knew he was looking into the jaws of hell.

The crow. Bertram.

The words floated through the air. He wasn't sure if he'd imagined them.

More words he didn't know. They resonated like those of the old language.

Morrigan. Bran. Y cysgod-cerddwr.

They made no sense in his delirium. He felt as if he was far away, cocooned, as some savage force tore at a distant barrier.

The crow.

He saw a shadow prowling a distant hillside. The palpable raw menace faded as it drew farther away.

Janet, clutching his hand. *Our baby,* she whispered.

A young boy, standing unafraid as wraiths twisted around him.

Something else. Something important. He couldn't understand what. He tried to look farther, to see what he had missed, but then everything faded away.

The first thing he felt was cold. So cold. A dull gray hue lingered around him.

Morning. He'd been there for hours. All night.

He struggled to sit up, shaking his head to clear the swirling fog. A raven was perched on the fold wall, watching him. It hopped a step closer. Bobbed its head, waiting. He clutched at his face in sudden panic.

Undamaged. He'd suffered no assault from their vicious beaks. He lowered his trembling hands.

There was something at his back. Soft. Furry.

Shep had lain next to him, in his hour of need, to lend him the warmth of his body. His heart swelled. His dear old friend, how had he known? He'd saved his life. He reached out to stroke his fur in thanks.

Then a sense of strangeness entered his mind. Something was wrong. His hand felt sticky. The fur was cold. Very cold.

Blinking hard, he managed to clear his vision. A half-open, glassy eye looked into his. One leg was almost torn away, a huge hole gaped in his side. The trail of red showed how far he'd crawled, in his dying moments, to reach his master's side.

Bert stared at him. He reached out to rub the stiff cold ears, then bowed his head and cried.

38

"Has he had any success, this Mr. Bigley?" Ellen was looking at Bert with obvious concern.

He shook his head. "Two weeks he's been here, and he's got nowhere. He'll never find anything."

He could hardly believe it. Two weeks.

Two weeks since it had taken Shep. Two weeks since he'd seen Thomas.

Hora fugit. The hour marches on.

"Don't be so disheartened, Uncle. This'll be sorted out." She put her hand on his shoulder. "Have something to eat, you're not looking well at all."

Bert sat down wearily, no strength to argue, and Ellen handed him a slab of fruitcake. "How many is it now?" she asked quietly.

"Too many."

But he'd give them all, just to have dear old Shep back. He stretched his hand down toward the floor out of long habit, but of course the comforting, soft nose wasn't there to touch his fingers any more. He snatched his hand up again and rubbed his eyes.

"What else is it, Uncle?" Ellen's gaze was shrewd. "There's something else as well, isn't there?"

What could he say? It was his responsibility to destroy it, but he'd tried and failed. It was a burden he couldn't hope to fulfill. Not now. He'd failed.

"It's nothing, lass." It wasn't right to tell her. She was only a woman. Barely even that. He still thought of her as a girl. And she had problems enough of her own.

"How's it with Jack?"

She seated herself on the settle. "He's trying to get more work, but it's not easy. And he drinks so much . . ."

She was looking tired. And very pregnant.

"I see he's been digging the garden, though." He tried to sound pleasantly enthusiastic.

"It was so I could grow flowers. I'd love to grow flowers. He said he'd get it ready for me. But he hasn't found time to touch it for weeks now." She could hardly keep the tremble from her voice.

A clamor outside. "They've found him! They've found him!"

He looked at Ellen and raised his eyebrows.

She shook her head and leaned back tiredly. "Must be Richard Pilcher. He never made it home two days ago. His wife was getting worried by last night. He usually manages to remember his way home by midmorning."

Through the window Bert could see a crowd massing. He obviously hadn't been found sleeping it off under a haystack.

He stood up wearily, the weight of guilt already gnawing in his chest. He would have to go and see. See what other horror was to be burdened on his failure. Ellen started to rise as well.

"No, you stay here, lass." It was no sight for a pregnant woman, whatever it was going to be.

"Uncle . . . ," she said, fixing him with worried eyes. "Please be careful. I don't want anything to happen to you."

He gazed at her, remembering his happy, perfect moment, already over a month ago. That faint candle in the darkness. He had to try and hold on to that feeling. He nodded. "I will, lass."

And he went out to join the crowd.

As he reached the corner someone dashed out and narrowly avoided colliding with him. Mick Pinkerley. He looked distraught when he saw who he'd nearly knocked over.

"Mr. Allenston . . ."

"Get out of the way, boy!"

The boy kept pace as he strode along. "Um, Mr. Allenston?"

Bert ignored him.

"I think something really bad might have happened."

"I know that, boy. Keep out of my way!"

"No, I mean . . ." His words were lost in the crowd.

A pair of young boys pushed through the legs of the adults, eager for a glimpse. Bert saw their grins fade, replaced by horror. One covered his mouth like he was going to be sick. He pushed his way through the throng, still clinging to the faint hope that the man had fallen. Maybe been struck by a cart.

But this was no accident. His throat, gaping and bloody, was testimony to that. His hands were red and torn where he'd tried, hopelessly, to fend it off. A single bloody footprint was left next to his face, taunting them. It was over six inches across.

"The wolf?" he heard someone whisper. Disbelieving, pathetic, hopeful.

A murmur spread. Everyone in town had lately had the sense of something lurking in the darkness, on the edges of rationality, but this was the first time it had made its presence so blatant.

He saw Mick stagger to one side and lose his breakfast in the ditch.

"Someone bring a cart!" Bert shouted. Pilcher may have been a drunkard, but he had a family. A widow. Three fatherless daughters. An infirm father. All destined for the poorhouse. Because of him.

He looked around the crowd, imagining their eyes on him, accusing and angry. And so they should. It was his fault.

He heard the motor car long before he saw it. That cursed hunter was coming. The crowd parted to allow the vehicle through, then closed behind it.

Bigley paused to carefully arrange his hat before climbing out. He swept a speck of dust from his jacket and strode toward Pilcher, swishing his cane to clear himself a path. No one backed away very far.

"Unfortunate, of course," he declared as he straightened up. "But if he will walk about at night, hopelessly drunk . . ." He turned aside.

A ripple of anger spread through the crowd. "When are you going to catch it?" someone shouted.

Bigley looked over the crowd, trying to ascertain who had spoken. "If any of you had the slightest understanding of wild beasts, of the intricacies of hunting big game—"

"Balderdash!"

"You've no idea!"

"Our livelihoods, our families!"

The crowd drew in closer. Bigley stepped back, glancing toward his motorcar. "I have set traps, lures, laid bait and poison. I have searched for lairs, trails, and prints. I've done my best," he finished lamely.

A ripple like thunder ran through his audience. Bigley took another two steps back until he reached the ditch bank, holding his cane defensively in front of him.

Bert went to his side. "Leave the man alone," he said quietly. "He's done his best, but he knows nothing about the fells. We all knew he'd get nowhere." There was no point taking it out on the ridiculously dressed fool.

Bigley glanced at him, bridling but wisely remaining silent.

People glanced at each other. Bigley took the opportunity to hurry through them to his motorcar, pulling his hat down farther over his face as if it would help him escape.

As the machine spat and smoked its way down the road, Bert noticed the Pinkerley boy again, staring at the cart on which Pilcher's body was being laid. His face was etched with horror, and something else. Guilt. Anyone would think he was responsible.

Bert looked up at the fells, at a kite soaring far up in the sky. What was he going to do now? He would have to try again. Carve yet another head. Perhaps this time—

"Mr. Allenston?"

"What?!"

Mick cringed, as if expecting a blow. Bert caught himself. He was only a boy, after all.

"What's the matter, Mick?" he asked, more kindly.

"Something terrible's happened." His face crumpled, and he was about to cry.

The boy worked in the mine now. In Hell's Mouth, Bert remembered Hilda telling him. And he'd been telling the children tales about monsters.

A sudden beam of hope shone into his mind.

39

Imbolc dawned. Halfway between the Long Night and the Equal Night of spring, it was the festival of birth and beginnings.

The tension in the air was audible to Bran's ears, more so than it had ever been before. A deep hum throbbed all around him and through the rocky ground beneath his feet, descending in waves to the village below. The earth herself was quivering with anticipation. Today was a new beginning in so many ways.

Nine months after Beltane. Beth's babe would be born today. It was also the full moon. His preparations were complete; his carving was finished. Today he would complete the binding ritual to imprison the cysgod-cerddwr.

He looked up at the Clenched Fist, the first rays of sun illuminating each finger. A beginning could only follow an ending. What was to end?

It would not be the Pridani. Bran nodded to himself as he weighed the leather bag in his hand. He could feel the power and energy of the wolf's head, despite it being well wrapped in wool, the only substance that would absorb or leach none of the infused magic.

He was ready. He breathed in the sharp Imbolc air and felt it surge through his body. He looked forward with calm confidence.

He banked the fire high so he would have warmth when he returned that night, then strode down the crisp hillside to the village.

Cowherds called their charges, children ran and squealed, skidding to a sedate walk as they passed him. The smell of baking bread lingered in the air and he could hear the rhythmic swish of querns on the grain.

He reached the Meeting Place, and soon everyone was gathered. Beth, with Coll's arm supporting her, looked exhausted, a sheen of sweat on her face. He watched her lean against Coll's bulk. Mintana stared at him, her face a mask of awe, then burst into tears. She quickly stifled her sobs.

Bran met the eyes of every one of the people under his leadership and guidance.

"Today is a new beginning. The beginning of the future." His words rang around the high walls.

He fell silent. There was no need to say more.

He saw something cross Beth's face, a wave of shock and pain. She cried out, clutching at Coll's arm. Her nails dug into his skin.

Her first birthing pain. Bran was surprised at his rush of feelings. The women were already gathering like a flock of sparrows. Beth gasped a deep breath as the pain passed.

Coll's thick arm was supporting her while he stared between her and Bran, his face stricken and helpless. Men were all the same.

"Coll, get her to the birthing hut. She will need support on the way."

The smith nodded quickly, masking his panic.

Bran placed his hands on Beth's shoulders and looked into her eyes. "The Goddess is at your side, Beth. She's watching over you."

She managed a quick smile before another pain took her. The women had gathered furs, water, absorbent moss, and everything else. A couple were already running towards Bride's Well to prepare a fire. The birthing hut had stood here for generations. The Maiden Goddess watched over all women as they left her ward and entered the wardship of the Mother.

"And Coll, don't worry."

As women fussed, men stood uncertainly, children pushed to see the start of this legendary event, Bran turned and walked from the village. A kite soared high over the Clenched Fist as he took to the path. Almost nobody saw him go.

40

"What do you know, Mick?" Bert fought the urge to shake the boy.

"You know those stories, that the devil was trapped in Hell's Mouth by a saint's prayers, hundreds of years ago?" The boy looked up nervously, searching his face for signs of encouragement.

"Yes, I know."

"I think we may have let him out." He shuffled from foot to foot. "We found something in the cave. Something happened, and then all this started. I think this is all our fault." His voice shook. A few people looked their way and Bert led him to one side.

"What did you find?"

"A stone head. It looked like a wolf. George Templeton found it. I told him not to touch it. It was evil, I could see that. But George, he picked it up. And something left it. It was alive, and then it was dead. And that's what's doing this, isn't it?"

Mick's eyes were fixed on him with something like terror. "That's why no one can kill it. Because it's the devil himself. No one believes me, but it's true, I swear it. You believe me, don't you? You know I've never lied to you. We've got to do something. We've got to stop it. What can we do, Mr. Allenston? What can we do?"

What could he do?

He looked up at the hillside. Some of Samuel Gatesby's sheep drifted in search of grass. Samuel was walking along the wall line, a gun under his arm.

"What happened to the head?"

"George took it home for his missus."

"I need to get it."

Mick nodded eagerly. "I'll go and see him. He said he owes me a favor. I covered for him when he had to go early when his missus was ill."

He hesitated for a moment. "You believe me, don't you? It is a monster doing this, not a wolf, isn't it?"

Bert was silent. But what was the point in denying it?

"Yes, it is."

Overhead, a raven squawked.

He waited in the market square for the boy to come back. A few people hurried across the cobblestones; others stood in groups, discussing the latest. He didn't want to talk to anyone, so he went and sat by the, well where he hoped he wouldn't be seen. He listened to the water trickling into the stone trough beside him.

He couldn't let himself get too hopeful. His idea would probably come to nothing. But he kept checking compulsively for the boy's return.

He was taking too long. He obviously couldn't get it. He watched the incessant ripples dancing across the trough for a moment, then saw the boy hurrying toward him.

Mick was holding something bundled in a leather bag. He stood. Mick pushed it toward him, then wiped his hands on his trousers.

It was heavy, and even through its shroud of cloth gave him an odd feeling. He fought an urge to drop it. He could see why Mick had wanted to get rid of it so quickly. He didn't dare unwrap it.

"What did he say, this Templeton?"

"He didn't want it anymore."

"Why not?"

"His missus, she didn't like it. It scared her."

A light flickered in his mind. A candle of hope.

"He said she was upstairs, airing the bed linen, and heard a noise on the landing. She looked out, thinking it's George, and saw a wolf there, standing on two legs. Huge, it was. Fangs like razors, bright blue eyes. She screamed and slammed the door, and then it walked down the stairs and vanished. When George got home she was still in there. The front door was shut, no way it could have got out, but it was gone. He thinks she's going crazy."

Mick glanced over his shoulder, then wiped his hands again, looking nervously at the package. "It went back to it. Why did it do that? Does it still live in it?"

The flicker of light grew stronger. That was exactly what Bert was thinking. The binding spell hadn't fully broken.

"Thanks, Mick. You've done a good job." He nodded and walked off.

It was six days until the next full moon. He knew what he had to do.

41

Bran saw the two figures long before they saw him. Down near the burn, trying to net trout, by the look of it. No fish at all up here, he could have told them. Two horses were nosing through the sedge with dismal hope.

They were dressed in the style of the invaders. A leather tunic, breeches, a helmet and an elaborate arrangement of metal plates that didn't seem to impede their movement at all. They were tall and powerful. Bran could sense a raw menace about them, like forged iron, hard and brutal.

What happened when dogs were chained? They grew fat and lazy, yes, but they also grew bored and restless.

He checked the sun again. He had to reach the cave well before sunset. Skirting around the treacherously boggy area to avoid them would take him well out of his way. But if he knew anything about bored young men, an encounter would take awhile. He could afford to do neither.

He turned left and carefully made his way across the marshy ground. Rivulets of brown water seeped up from under his boots. He reached an outcrop and looked back. The two men were watching him.

He knew they would follow him. He hurried on with a curse. They were on horseback. He was on foot. He had an obvious advantage.

He chose his path carefully, leading deeper into the bog. The ground tugged greedily at his boots with each step. He was going far out of his way, but he couldn't let them follow him to the cave.

He looked back again. They'd reached the bad ground already but were struggling to steer their mounts through the treacherous peat. Over this type of ground, it was far quicker on foot. That was how the raiding parties in the south achieved such success.

One of the horses stumbled. Its rider fell with a strange-sounding curse. He struggled but couldn't free himself from the mud. The other rider jumped down to help, sinking to his shins himself. Bran grinned as he hurried along the barely visible path to the next rise. He could see why they were so desperate to build their roads. He would soon be well away from them. He checked the sun again as he jogged on.

The sun was less than two fingers' width from the horizon when he finally reached the cave. The full moon was about to emerge. When both were equal and opposite, when day and night were both and neither there, at the time between times, energy poured through the land in a mighty torrent. It would empower his soul.

But it would also empower the beast and shatter the constraint he'd laid across the cave half a moon earlier.

He had enough time. He began to lay out his circle. He fixed a piece of twine to the ground with a rock, stretched it out, and traced a six-pace ring in front of the cave, marking it out with ground chalk and salt. The two white rocks—the color of sacrifice.

Then he measured two triangles with equal length sides within the circle, superimposed to form a six-pointed star. The three sacred shapes; they could concentrate and bind the most powerful energies known. Powerful enough to force the cysgod-cerddwr into its prison.

At each point of the star, Bran placed a small wooden bowl filled with beeswax, a reed wick in the center. When lighted, they would act as a microcosm of the light of the soul, in the presence of which the blackness of the beast's own soul would be helpless.

Checking the sun again, he began to unwrap the totems of the Pridani, and of the earth on which they depended. A branch of silver birch, the buds already forming. As he placed it at the northern point, he saw in his mind the leaves bursting free. The first step of the cold, dead forest as it moved toward summer.

The rowan, the berries still clinging on. He saw shadows jerk back as he moved it to the second point. The air shimmered around it as its magic rose in an invisible veil.

The berries gleamed blood-red under the dying sun. The color of death. The color of birth. The Druids called the rowan the Quickening Tree.

Third, the hawthorn. The tree of the Goddess, of Beltane. The tree that guards the veil between worlds. As he laid it down, it took root and flourished. White blossoms dazzled in the sun. Beneath its boughs, an emptiness lingered in the air. It flickered as something slipped through. A soul, into the land of birth. Before long, another returned.

Fourth, the hazel. He placed nine nuts in a square. The ground shimmered and split beneath them. Water flowed through the crevice, bringing with it a colossal silver salmon, which gulped the nuts down.

Bran touched a finger to its scales. The image vanished. The nuts lay on the ground as he'd placed them.

The hazel was the tree of wisdom.

Fifth, the heather. The haunt of late-summer bees. He heard them humming as they foraged. Saw them gathering nectar, nurturing their brood and the queen in their midst. Infusing their honey with their harmony and magic to produce the most sacred food.

And finally, the oak. He saw the mighty tree, standing proud through the storm. Its leaves clung on until the Cailleach unleashed her full power to tear them from the boughs. The oak marked the death of the year, the end that came before the beginning.

And at the very center of it all, the pivot point around which everything was created, he placed the stone head.

He stood at the top of the circle and concentrated. Closed his eyes and let the energies flow and eddy around him, rippling over his skin like the faintest of breezes.

Something didn't feel right. He opened his eyes and scanned over his work. It was perfect; he'd done nothing wrong. He concentrated again.

Something was definitely wrong. He felt ever so slightly off balance. A pressure as the energy current built up against one side of the circle. The reason struck him with a palpable cold blow.

He'd chosen the wrong place.

42

Bert planted his feet firmly in the center of his pentagram, then raised his arms to the sky. The stone head filled the clearing around St. Bride's Well with some strange, alien presence. The ritual drink drove away the biting chill, and the dizziness he'd felt the first time was mingled with elation. This time he would succeed.

The feeling grew more palpable as it spread through his body. An ancient magic, powerful and frightening, filled him. A glimpse of the last time this had been done. He felt the calm, grim confidence and that feeling mingled with his own spirit. When it reached his fingertips and his toes, he opened his eyes.

Light radiated from his mind to fill the circle, spreading out in waves and rebounding from the points of the pentagram. Myriad ripples shimmered all around him. He could feel the light penetrating deep into the earth and rising high into the sky.

With his newfound awareness, he could feel the dark warm earth beneath the frost. Already, life was stirring. Seeds were beginning to germinate, far below the surface. Slowly, slowly, beginning to push upward, long before the first warm days of spring would herald their arrival. He could feel the roots of the trees tentatively drawing up moisture, rising through the trunks and branches to reach the thousands of twigs that would soon burst into life.

The vitality disguised within the sleeping forest coursed through his body and soul. As the power of man combined with that of the earth, he became a part of it all.

He watched the multicolored tendrils flow outward from the stone carving, the perfect likeness of a wolf's head. Many of the threads had snapped, frayed, withered into dullness, but he'd been right. Some were still intact. They shimmered outward to disappear into the darkness, into the void that was already circling around him.

He reached out with his mind and pulled one of the broken threads. It stretched, flickered, but remained intact. He wrapped it around the void as it prowled past.

It resisted, pulled back from his touch, but the thread held. The pressure against the circle grew slightly heavier.

Bert didn't let himself feel anything. It was going to be harder this time. It understood. It wouldn't be fooled twice. He held his mind steady, smooth as a mirror reflecting the light of the earth, and gradually he repaired more threads.

The bonds grew stronger. When he thought he'd done enough, he began to pull. It fought hard, but he didn't waver.

The wind rose. Branches thrashed about, the leaf litter was swirling around him, but he didn't break his concentration. A crack as a branch fell, thudding onto the frozen ground. He drew the beast in farther.

It reached the edge of the circle, the point where he'd failed before. Again the resistance was too great.

For the first time, the mirror of his mind began to waver. What would happen when he got it past the barrier? What would stop it simply tearing him to pieces?

His grip was weakening. The void was gaining strength. Another branch fell, this time just feet behind him. He jumped. One of the threads frayed and snapped.

He took a deep, calming breath and the mirror stilled. The light remained intact. He was in control. He was in control and the beast could not harm him. He ignored the broken thread. The others were more than enough.

The raven's feathers in the pentagram were floating upward. He had the impression that the five pieces of wood were growing. The air shimmered as invisible branches burst through it.

Ravens circled above him. The constant pulse of wings echoed through his mind, together with the throbbing light. He began to feel like he was floating, rising up on the current of sound. He didn't dare disturb the spell by looking down.

He pulled the threads tight. They steadily drew into the head. He held the beast firmly against the ring of light, and began to intone the binding formula. The words that would imprison it forever.

"Dewch, cysgwch, llonydd am erioed," he recited through the entire invocation.

It was closer, weaker. But he could sense something else. A discordance, a flicker of disharmony.

Something was wrong.

43

Bran's heart rate began to surge. His careful preparations were worthless. Everything had to be perfect else the beast would destroy him in an instant. That slight imbalance would magnify until everything he'd achieved would shatter under the pressure.

He forced his emotions under control. He willed his heartbeat and his shaking hands to calm, then swept up all his preparations. He glanced to the west. The sun was almost touching the distant hillside.

He studied the ground in front of the cave. Everywhere he could now perceive that slight undercurrent. A subtle imbalance of the natural energy, all through the area, prickling like a gentle breeze against his skin. Why had he not noticed that before?

With a grudging respect, he realized the cysgod-cerddwr must be somehow responsible. It had masked his awareness. For a while. Bran smiled grimly. He was still more than a match for it.

He would have to go inside the cave. There was no other option. Underground, the currents were masked by the bedrock; he would find the perfectly balanced space he needed. He stepped down into the darkness.

It was cold, unnaturally so. And the darkness was absolute. The rapidly dying light from outside vanished almost immediately. The cysgod-cerddwr was not finished yet.

Bran could sense he was in a cavern, with great space to each side and above. The slight scuffling of his footsteps echoed back from all around him. He slowed his pace, treading carefully.

A sound ahead. Like the scratch of claws on rock. Like a faint intake of breath. He ignored it.

The echoes were coming closer together: the cavern was narrowing. Then he met a rocky wall. He felt his way along it and found the mouth of a new tunnel. Around his height and three paces across. Emanating from it, an acrid chill prickled at his face. He concentrated on the swirling eddies he could feel and drew a slow breath. This was the spot.

A faint brush of movement on his cheek. It could have been a flurry of falling dust. He groped for the first of the candles then struck his flint.

The flare of orange was blinding. Then his eyes adjusted and he pivoted, holding the light outwards. It penetrated deep into the gloom. He could see nothing but emptiness.

He forced himself to concentrate as he repeated his preparations then placed the stone head in the center. He removed its woolen covering, careful not to touch the stone, and then stood in the circle and waited.

Sunset passed. The moon rose. Although he could see nothing of the outside world, his heightened senses told him that. The moon would now be a half hand's width above the eastern horizon, and the sun was well on its way beneath the earth.

It didn't come.

Bran remained relaxed. Fear would be his undoing. It would come, he knew. He concentrated on the air flowing through his lungs.

A force struck him, almost knocking him from his feet. He could see nothing but blackness, nothing but nothing. But the emptiness was now alive.

He struggled to regain his balance and focused on the flickering lights, the points where he knew they would be. They were still burning. Slowly they reemerged from the abyss.

He stilled his mind and then began to push the beast back, driving it back into the tunnel. Beads of sweat broke out on his forehead. He began to shake.

Something gave way. The cysgod-cerddwr retreated. Its presence no longer touched him but it entirely surrounded the ring. It couldn't pass, and neither could Bran leave the circle. There was no way out for either of them.

They waited.

Bran filled his lungs with air, as deep as he could. He exhaled, then breathed again. Three times he repeated the action, feeling a sparkling energy fizzing through his being. Sparks of light like thousands of Dying Stars appeared, emerging from one rocky wall and penetrating the other. The candles burned brighter as the surging energy fed them.

The beast retreated into the cave and Bran propelled it back farther.

He began to sing. The song of the earth, the song of life. The song of all things that are, and were, and will be. The song with which the world was sung into being.

As eons of time flowed through the cave, an endless night was shattered by a burst of light. A dimly seething primeval sea gave up the first living things. Blasts of fire erupted from the ground. A Fiery Star plummeted. Flame spread across the world, and new seeds kindled from the charred remains.

Bran felt alive, in a way he'd never felt before. He knew what it meant to be a part of the world. The legacy of all time burst into his soul and he longed to scream with ecstasy.

Then he saw her. The Goddess, as dazzling as the summer ocean, as delicate as the nascent moon. She turned red as blood as her essence surged through the soul of the world. Through its rivers, lakes, and seas. Through the veins of man and beast. Through the stems of plant and tree.

At her side, her son, the Horned God of the Green. As Bran beheld him, he saw within him the entirety of the life that the Goddess had birthed. He looked on for an eternity as countless lives grew and flourished, then withered and died as the Goddess transformed into her third and final face. He watched their deaths seed lives anew.

He saw a hawk seize a finch midair. Its brood of chicks tear greedily at the still-warm flesh.

He saw the King Stag drag himself away from the field, head held low, blood dripping from his wounds, as the victor bellowed and charged toward the waiting hinds.

Her final aspect, black and terrible. He could feel her daring him to look upon her. He met her eyes with confidence. A terrible, unconquerable, indefinable power, he felt himself falling into the pools of swirling blackness.

He steadied his balance. Centered and focused, he gazed on her face. She nodded, a slow smile on her face.

Life. Death. They were one and the same. He realized her real purpose behind the Clenched Fist.

This truth locked in his heart, he turned to the darkness and drew the cysgod-cerddwr toward him. He pulled on the threads snaking out from his mind to entwine it. It was taken by surprise and he made rapid progress.

Then it began to fight. He got it to the edge of the circle, but his energy was weakening. The effort was too much. He hung on.

One of the bonds snapped. A candle was extinguished in an explosion of darkness. The circle of light was broken.

It was over. He'd lost. His mind was breached, his faith wounded. The cysgod-cerddwr knew that at once. And instead of struggling, it attacked.

44

Bert repeated the entire formula again, but the discord grew more palpable. Had he remembered one of the words wrong?

The void moved nearer. What was missing?

The mirror of light began to waver. The darkness pressed inward.

The words sounded unbidden from the pool of his mind. *A skylark sings in the face of danger.*

He saw again the bird exploding up from under his feet that long ago morning, what seemed a lifetime ago. And the answer came to him. He was meant to *sing* the ritual.

His grandfather had never told him that, but in his heart he knew it was right. It had been forgotten over the years, but the answer had somehow managed to find him.

His voice was harsh—he'd never sung in his life—but his song gained its own momentum. He sang the song of the lark, the wind in the heather, the scent of the moorland air. The first flakes of snow in winter, the swallow swooping overhead on its thousand-mile journey, the perpetual sound of grazing. The foraging bee, the kite rising on a thermal, a pair of lambs at their mother's udder, the shepherd on his watch. The song of the moors, the eternal cycle of life.

Carried on the notes of his song, he flew back through eons of time. He saw generations come and go. Men built dwellings of wattle and turf, precarious on the fell side. They watched their sheep, they grew old and died. The heather sprouted, flourished, withered, and sprouted. Battles were fought and lost. Settlements were razed and rebuilt. A babe was born in a rush of blood.

As he gazed at Janet's exhausted face, as her eyes turned toward his, at last he felt peace. It hadn't gone wrong. It was the way it was meant to be.

He saw that old ewe again, sent to the butcher all those months ago.

"That ewe with the broken horn's her daughter."

"That's nice. That means there's something left of her when she goes, doesn't it?"

Thomas had realized that, better than himself.

He reached out and took Janet's hand. Forty years of guilt and failure were swept away in a heartbeat as she squeezed his fingers and smiled. He finally understood.

A man in a raven-feathered cloak, strong and wise. His cloak handed to a beautiful, flame-haired woman. He saw a line of people, kneeling, looking up in smoldering hatred as blood dripped from their many wounds. Behind them, a village was burning.

But the people always returned. Like the sheep, they would always find their way home.

And so it went on, the ebb and flow of life, until it finished with a young boy sitting on his grandfather's knee.

The song died away. But it remained, echoing through the hills. The song of silence. The song of life. The song of eternity.

With a sudden implosion, the darkness was gone. The ground quaked and the stone head tumbled into the spring.

Bert slumped to the ground, exhausted. The transcendent light left him. He looked through the water into the beast's eyes. The malevolent glitter was at once terrifying and utterly exhilarating.

He'd done it.

45

The cysgod-cerddwr hurtled toward Bran, just as he'd wanted a heartbeat before. It broke straight through the circle. The momentum knocked him off balance. Terror took over.

He flung his arms up as he fell and felt something slash into his arms and face. A warm stickiness began to run into his eyes and mouth. It caught in his throat as he tried to gasp a breath.

There was no light now. The blackness had overwhelmed it. Whether the candles still burned, it no longer mattered. Teeth sank deep into his arm and his side but he was barely aware of the pain. The beast began to shake him.

As even that began to fade, he became dimly aware of something else. A rush of air on his face.

Wings.

He dropped to the ground. The raven squawked as it attacked and the beast turned its fury toward it.

The bird tore at its eyes, his beak gouging at the sharp blue orbs. His wings flapped furiously and the beast roared.

Bran's mind grasped for the remaining lights, still burning despite everything, and pulled himself back to the battle. With the last of his mental strength he threw more bands of energy around the beast. Preoccupied with the assailing raven, it didn't react until too late. It was ensnared in the center of the circle.

Bran forced his pain into the recesses of his mind. The beast thrashed and writhed. The roof of the cave began to fall.

He was shaking, mind and body. With the last shreds of his strength, he forced the cysgod-cerddwr inward, towards the stone head. He could feel blood pouring from his nose and mouth as he struggled to breathe.

With one last desperate effort, he screamed and forced the beast backward, downward, inward. Stone and dust fell all around, choking his lungs and stinging his eyes. He was dimly aware of a deep, violent roar in his ears. Then he collapsed.

After one breath he forced himself to his knees. Where was it? He looked around in a daze.

Gone.

Stone and dust were still raining all around him but he stared toward the stone head. Its eyes flickered and pulsed. They were alive.

He'd done it.

He reached out to pick it up, his mind still reeling, but his Druid's sixth sense jerked his hand back. A faint buzz reaching toward his fingertips, a leaking of energy from the stone.

Something of its soul was not entirely trapped. If he touched it, it would be freed. The terrible thought ripped through his mind.

What should he do? He must bury it, somewhere where it could never be found.

A low rumble solved his problem. The cave was collapsing. Gods be good, it would bury the thing forever. He forced himself to his knees, managed to stand.

He staggered halfway across the cavern, the dim light of morning already penetrating its depths.

He fell. Behind him the rumble grew louder. Something struck him, then rolled away. He was aware of no pain now, just a creeping numbness. He dragged himself on. More debris buffeted him. Somehow, he kept moving.

Sunlight touched his face. Nearly there. With a screeching roar, the entire cave system collapsed. With his face to the dirt, the explosion passed above him. His ears rang, then fell silent. His mouth was filled with grit.

He realized he was outside, his face resting on cool grass. He closed his eyes and concentrated on his breathing. The cold air helped clear his lungs and his mind. After a while he was able to sit up. Long practice sharpened his thoughts.

He inspected the wounds to his body. Already his flesh was turning black and gangrenous. The beast had corrupted his body. He lay down again, watching the sun rising high. The light he would soon join.

He drifted, peaceful and quiet on the tides of time. Nearly there now. Shadows writhed about him, touched him with form-less fingers. The debt was paid.

He saw Coll taking his cloak, the next Pennaeth, until he handed the cloak to a beautiful, flame-haired woman. Beth's daughter.

He saw him provoke a war against the invaders. He saw them fighting back, relentless, until the land fell under the might of their swords.

He saw a line of people, kneeling, looking up in smoldering hatred as blood dripped from their many wounds. Behind them, a village was burning.

This wasn't meant to happen. He couldn't let it happen. He had to warn them.

With an immense effort, he focused. Got to his knees, and then his feet.

Near the cave he found two sticks, and he began the long, slow struggle back to the village.

He had no idea how much time passed. The slow tramp of his feet, over and over. Over and over. Keep going. He just had to keep going.

He reached the stream. A few mouthfuls of spring water refreshed him a little, washed some of the corruption from his soul. He struggled on.

The sun was almost setting by the time he reached the village, although his eyes and mind had grown dark long ago. He could barely make out the causeway across the ditch, and he dropped to his knees as he tried to concentrate. As the gates were dragged open and footsteps ran toward him, he heard a faint wailing sound, far in the distance. The cry of a newborn babe.

46

What now? Bert had to make sure the secret was preserved, that someone would remember the story and the ritual. One day the time would come again.

He looked up at the full moon, flickering through the bare branches. It silhouetted an array of hazel catkins, the first hint of spring in the cold, sleeping wood.

But who could he tell? Thomas was a child of the new century; he would forget the old ways. He wouldn't even believe the story, let alone remember it.

Perhaps Ellen's bairn. Of all the Allenstons he could tell, his mind kept drawing back to her. Hopefully the child would be a boy. He smiled ruefully. The Feltons, of all people, carrying on the onus of generations.

He wondered about telling Ellen herself, but dismissed the thought immediately. He knew he could never do that.

But anyway, it probably didn't matter. No one would find the wolf's head here anyway. When had the girls last come to St. Bride's Well in search of their sweetheart? Not for years. And why would they? They had parties, dances, all sorts of gaiety. They never had to look as far as this. Today was St, Bride's feast day, and still no one had come except him. It seemed both fitting and ironic that the ritual had taken place today.

He got to his feet, leaning against an ash sapling for balance as dizziness swam over him. The sapling swayed under his weight as he steadied himself. Ready to harvest next autumn, he vaguely thought. Ideal for wheel spokes.

He waited a moment for his mind to clear, then began to walk back through the trees. The moon was well risen and he could see his way clearly, but he stumbled more than once. He was glad he'd remembered to pick up his crook.

He made it to the road and began to walk up the incline. At least the road was relatively even here. He was desperate for a hot drink and his fireside.

"Uncle! What are you doing out here?"

He looked around in confusion. Of course, Ellen lived here now, in Mrs. Tipping's old cottage. He'd forgotten for a moment.

She was standing on her doorstep, looking pale and pregnant in the moonlight.

"Lass, what are you doing out, this time of night?"

Of course, waiting for her husband to return from the tavern. First of February today. He'd have been paid. Bert swayed slightly.

Her eyes bored into his face. "Are you all right, Uncle? You don't look well. Are you still worrying about the wolf?"

"That Bigley's got nowhere," he said evasively. Her gaze didn't waver.

"I think the problem will be sorted soon," he added uncomfortably. Ellen was very sharp. He had the feeling she knew exactly what had been going on.

A screech in the road ahead. They both looked at the raven hopping toward the trees. It was trailing a wing.

"What's it doing out in the dark? Poor thing—must be injured."

The bird turned. Bert felt a frisson of recognition.

"Where have you been, Uncle?"

He forced himself to turn back to her. "Just out for a walk, down by the dene."

She immediately looked concerned. "By that old spring? I saw someone had been down there."

He started. Had he been wrong? Perhaps she was the one he should tell. Suddenly, he felt he must.

Her eyes fixed on his, gentle and urging. He could feel the words rising into his mind. He steeled himself.

"It's nothing. It's been a long day; I need to get home."

She nodded silently. As he walked away, he could feel her eyes burning into his back. The raven squawked again, almost despairing. The sound tugged inside him, making him long to turn back.

But he knew he'd done the right thing.

He had no idea how long it took him to reach home. He managed to kindle a fire from the cold ashes, then shivered and rubbed his hands. It was so cold in here tonight! The feeling that had come over him earlier had got worse. The chafing of his hands left a queer tingling in his skin which began to intensify.

He stood up, clutched the back of his chair as his legs betrayed him, then struggled to the fireplace. He threw three more logs on, but they did nothing to ease the chill in the room.

He sat down, shut his eyes for a moment. He was surprised to see the room had blurred. He blinked and rubbed his eyes, but couldn't focus at all. The tingling in his arms became a sharp, stabbing pain. He gasped but his breath caught painfully in his throat. With a huge effort he willed himself to relax.

His chest freed and he managed to draw a breath. He recalled the death of his uncle, Ellen's grandfather. They'd said his heart had given out.

He opened his eyes and saw the room had grown darker. Resignation, sadness, regret. He would never see Ellen's unborn child. He would never pass on the secret.

Outside he could hear a ewe's blart. It was Molly, he could tell. Soft and whickering; she knew. *Good-bye.*

He felt like he was falling. There was a soft breeze around his skin and the pain was wafted away. He could smell tobacco, the rich pungent stuff that his grandfather had smoked, and instantly he was drawn back into the long-gone past.

It was light now, an effusive gentle glow bathed the room. His grandfather was leaning on his crook, his cap at its usual angle.

Well done, boy. He felt his unspoken words. His grandfather held out his hand, gnarled, weathered, and cracked, and he reached up to grasp it.

Then he pulled back. He hadn't completed his task. His knowledge, the secret, generations old, it was going to die with him. That couldn't happen. The darkness returned, and with it the searing pain.

His grandfather shook his head, his hand stretched out with more urgency. *There's nothing left to do. It's time.*

Bert let his heart fill with peace. His young soft fingers, years away from the toil of the shepherd's life, grasped hold of his grandfather's. Molly and his other girls would be well cared for. Thomas would see to that. He could hear them all now, their voices joined with Molly, then the sound faded into the rush of air.

His last thought formed in his mind before too fading into silence.

God help those who were to come.

Epilogue

The years passed. The world began to change. Countries rose and fell. Wars were lost and won.

In Allendale, life too began to change. People looked to the future. The old ways were forgotten. Obscured by the fug of coal smoke and rock dust, the rich folklore and heritage of the fells, once so carefully cherished, was lost forever.

The Wolf of Allendale became nothing but an occasionally told children's story. The song of silence was heard no more.

Around St. Bride's Well, the woods were no longer harvested as factories replaced the woodland crafts, and so the trees grew tall and strong. Their roots sucked greedily at the ground water and the ancient spring began to weaken.

Autumn after autumn, leaves shrouded the forgotten and untended spring. Reduced to a trickle, it forced its way up through the leaf litter until, one hot dry summer, it lost its battle for survival.

Barnaby gazed around as the three boys reached the top of the rise, drinking in the purple swaths of heather he wouldn't see again. The only sound above their panting was the wind plowing across miles of fells, just like in the old days they'd learned about in school.

Then a chainsaw fired up down in the wood and the illusion was shattered.

In a field half a mile away, a tractor was busy harrowing. A few seagulls followed behind. A kite drifted overhead on a thermal and then floated down to the rocky outcrop shaped like a hand, landing on the fore finger. So familiar, so normal, so *home*. His eyes blurred and a strangled sob escaped his mouth.

"Hey, come on, Barn! Boarding school won't be that bad! Think of the midnight feasts, and you'll be back home at Christmas." Trevor Felton looked at him with mixed sympathy and concern.

"I wish I didn't have to go! Mam doesn't want me to either. I heard her say eight's too young, but Grandfather says I've got to."

Barnaby slumped to the ground and started pulling handfuls of grass. Freezing dorms. Gruel. Bullies. The cane. He wished he could run away into the hills and never go back.

"That's what you get for having a rich family. Everyone says the Allenstons are really loaded." Trevor pulled a paper bag of sweets from his pocket and handed one to Barnaby. He silently took it.

"Your family can't do anything but what your grandfather says, can you?" Robert Pinkerley sat down next to him.

"He was supposed to be a shepherd; we were all shepherds back then. But he got a scholarship to Hexham Grammar School, and now he owns four iron foundries. He says the only way you get anywhere in life is through damned hard work, and that's what he expects from all of us."

Tears began to flood down his cheeks. "Dad had to go to boarding school, and Uncle Godwin, and now we do too. It's not fair!"

"At least I'll never have to go," said Trevor. "Dad said I'm not to get no fancy ideas, not on his pittance of a wage."

After a few moments' silence, Robert stood up. "Let's go down to that wood and build a den. It'll be ready for when you come home, Barnaby."

"I don't know. Granny Ellen told me never go down there," said Trevor, looking down at the brooding swath of dark green. "The dene's dangerous."

"Why? It's just a wood, the same as all the others. Or are you frightened there might be ghosts? Or that monster my grandpa told us about last Christmas? The one that came out of the mine, ages ago? Don't be silly, glow in the dark!"

Trevor scrambled to his feet. "I'll smack you if you call me that again."

"All right then, Ginger! Carrots! Sunset!"

"Perhaps you should listen to her, Trev. You won't get any more sweets." Barnaby didn't really want to go down there either. He only had a few hours left now.

"'Course I will," Trevor countered. "I'm her favorite."

"'Cause he's the only carrottop, isn't that right? She hoped you'd all look like her." Robert danced out of reach of his kick.

"She's just lonely, Mam says. Has been since Grampy died. And if I go and see her I don't have to listen to that boring, soppy story again about how they fell in love and got married, even though everyone hated Grampy. Just like the stories in her boring, soppy books." He stuck his tongue out. "Come on, Barn. We're going to the wood."

They passed a derelict building after a few hundred yards, the roof long caved in, the walls crumbling, gaping holes where the door and windows had been. The adjoining barn had fared little better. A stone gate post, rusted hinges still attached, stood lonely among a line of rubble. Trevor glanced at the place curiously.

"I wonder who used to live there?"

The boys clambered over fallen stones in the doorway and looked around. The interior was bare, just stones and roof timbers were scattered across the floor. A rabbit disappeared into the rubble.

Only a rusty old stove and two jutting stones holding a rough-hewn shelf betrayed any sense that someone had once lived here. A big tree branch had grown across where the roof beam had once been, stretching out to touch the far wall. A rowan, they could tell from the jagged leaves.

The silent atmosphere seemed odd to Barnaby, almost familiar. "Imagine living here," he said.

He wished he could do that. Live as a shepherd like they used to. Never have to go to boarding school, never have to leave Allendale at all. It brought a lump of despair to his throat.

He picked his way over to the shelf, stretched up, and riffled through an inch of brittle leaf cover, twigs, and dust. Nothing. Although hundreds of hands had probably searched there before, he still felt disappointed.

As he turned back, he slipped on the precarious mound of rubble and dislodged a flurry of stones as he fell back onto his elbows.

"You all right, Barn?"

He noticed a funny-looking stone under the rubble. He picked it up and dusted it off, realizing at once it was a piece of carved horn. He turned it over and over. It looked strangely familiar, although he couldn't think why.

"What's that you've got?" Trevor came over to him. "A bird? A partridge or a grouse or something."

Of course! That finely carved stick in his grandfather's house, in the entrance hall where he kept his shooting sticks. Barnaby loved looking at it. The only nice thing in the house. He could just imagine it turning to look at him, bending to preen its breast feathers.

He stared at the carving in his hand. Its only flaw was its beak, which was skewed to one side.

"Barn! Hurry up! Robert's already gone."

He slipped the carving into his pocket and hurried out.

Two huge planes roared overhead, followed quickly by four more, and all three stopped to gape.

"Dad says there'll be war soon." Barnaby stared up at the rapidly dispersing smoke trail. "He says the West will never be reconciled with Communism, and war's all they're planning for in the Ministry."

"I hope they don't invade us," said Trevor fervently. "Imagine our fells, all mud and barbed wire and soldiers in trenches."

Barnaby shook his head. "It won't be like that. War's different now. They've got bombs. Big bombs. Those planes might even have been carrying them. Dad says they can blow a whole country to nothing. That's why we've got to go to war."

The others looked around, trying to imagine.

"Come on then," said Robert at last. "I've got to be home for tea soon."

The wood felt cold compared to the parched moor, and the three boys fell silent as they stepped over fallen branches and scrub. Trevor glanced uneasily over his shoulder. Why had Granny Ellen warned him away from this place?

Something tugged at his sleeve and he tore his arm away, a hole opening up in his sleeve as the briar snagged the wool. "Oh no! Mam'll be furious; she's sick of mending our things!"

Barnaby carefully untangled him. "We've got loads of old jumpers and things, just put in the attic. I'll bring you one tomorrow."

Trevor didn't reply, and he immediately realized why. There would be no tomorrow. He couldn't believe he'd forgotten.

Robert went on ahead and then turned back, grinning. Among a clump of ash trees was a natural rocky alcove. "Here's perfect! Just what we need!"

Trevor and Barnaby went up to join him. A raven squawked and flapped toward them. Barnaby flinched.

"These big rocks can be the walls, here's the way in, it's like a room already! We just need some branches to roof it, then it's done."

"I don't know. I don't like it." Barnaby hung back. "I think we should go back."

Trevor glanced at him, then stared silently at the alcove.

Robert raised his eyes skyward, then began to scrape away the leaf litter and twigs with his boot. He yelped as he kicked something hard. Kneeling down, he scraped in the soft ground. He picked something up and brushed it off.

Its teeth were bared fiercely. The glittering eyes seemed to stare gleefully at them. Barnaby stepped back instinctively.

"It's a dog!" Robert said in surprise.

"No," said Trevor with all the superior wisdom of his ten years. "Look how its ears are pricked straight up. It's not a dog. It's a wolf."

Glossary

Annwfn (*AN-yooven*) The dark regions of the Celtic otherworld.

bairn Northumberland word for child or baby.

bellwether The lead sheep of the flock.

Beltane A Celtic festival held on May 1 marking the sacred union of God and Goddess as the natural world flourishes, now called May Day.

blarting The sound of sheep.

boggle An otherworldly being that could either perform helpful tasks or play mischievous tricks on people.

bothy A shepherd's home.

Cailleach (*CAL-yak*) The Goddess in her winter or crone guise, literally meaning 'old woman.'

clarted up Covered in mud.

cysgod-cerddwr (*CUS-god CER-thor*) Shadow-walker.

ewe lamb A female sheep under a year old.

Howay A traditional Northumberland greeting.

Imbolc A Celtic festival of birth and new beginnings celebrated on February 1, now called St. Bride's Day or Candlemas.

Orion A constellation depicted as a huntsman in many cultures.

otherworld The world bordering our own, the destination of all souls after death and the home of spiritual or supernatural entities.

Pennaeth (*PEN-yth*) Leader or headman.

pipit A moorland songbird.

quern A set of stones for grinding grain.

rum 'un A sly or roguish person.

Samhain (*SA-wen*) A Celtic festival held on November 1 marking the start of winter and the day when the barriers between this world and the otherworld weaken, now called All Souls' Day or Halloween.

About the Author

HANNAH SPENCER is the author of *The Story of Light* (Moon Books, 2014) and numerous short stories that have been published by *Cracked Eye, Penny Shorts, Bewildering Stories, Writing Magazine*, and *Writers' Forum*. Between writing, Hannah Spencer works on a dairy sheep farm in Warwickshire, England. Visit her online at hannah-spencer-author.weebly.com.

CPSIA information can be obtained
at www.ICGtesting.com
Printed in the USA
LVHW032005231118
598050LV00006B/70/P

9 780062 674616